Imen of Atlantis

RUTHLESS

Volume Two

S.K.R.
&
TONY D'URSO

Imen of Atlantis: Ruthless

Editor: Tony D'Urso

ISBN: 978-0-9817679-4-9 (paperback)
ISBN: 979-8-89079-230-3 (ebook)

Cover: Viking warrior symbol for ruthless; rage

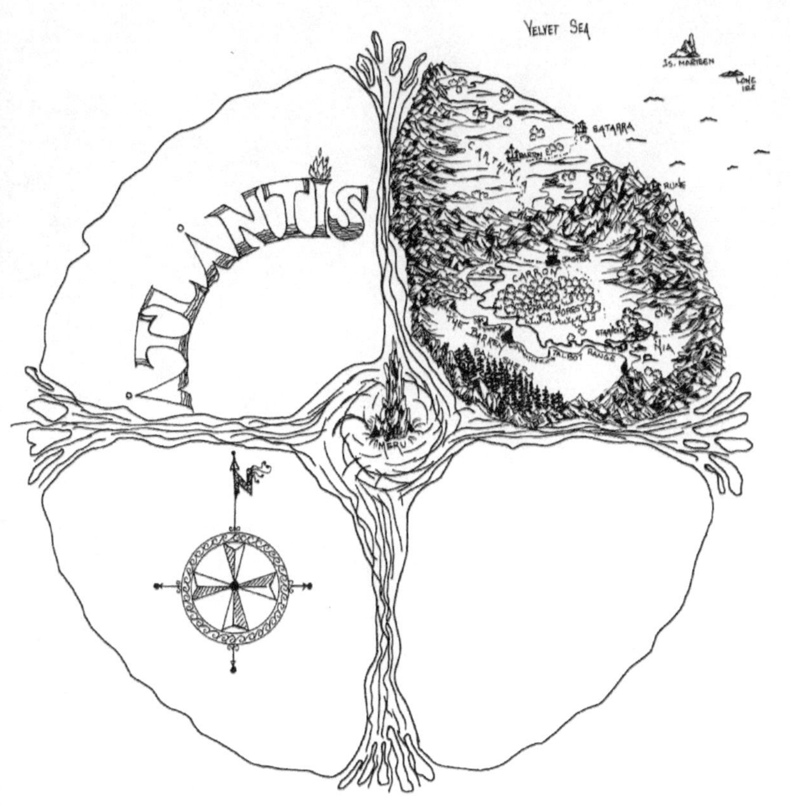

YELVET SEA
ATLANTIS
IS. MARYBEN
LONE ISLE
SATARRA
BARTON BOG
CARTHY
RUNE
JASPER
CARRON
CARRON FOREST
THE BARREN
TALBOT RANGE
STARRON
HIA
AMERUN

PROLOGUE

UNBEKNOWNST TO THE REST and isolated from the surface dwellers, in a subterranean world, the mystical race of Imen live a peaceful life, finding happiness within themselves and their community. They do not interact with anyone but do come to the surface occasionally, pulled by the call from nature and what the Creator ordained them for. This tale is all about them and more.

It is in these forests of Carron that the crux of the story first unfolds with a wild boar hunt by Prince Eyvind, the heir to the throne of Carron and the eldest son of King Audun and the Commander of Imperial Knights, along with his friends Raidon, Axel, and Laris. As dusk settles in, Eyvind leads the hunt with his arrow ready to strike at a boar. Unfortunately, stumbling on a gnarly tree root, the arrow is misdirected, and the boar is hit, not killed. Enraged, it charges toward Eyvind and gores his right thigh, leaving a gaping wound that bleeds heavily. Eyvind collapses and starts to fade in and out of consciousness.

Silent prayers are sent to the heavens above, and they are answered by the ethereal Imen, Roni and her two friends, Suki and Kenji, who live beneath the forest floor. They make their way through the Boad trees to where Eyvind lies injured and heal him. The men are left stunned.

Eyvind is thankful to Roni and is also completely enamored by her. And the feeling is reciprocated. But she crosses the rule of Imen and uses her gift to satisfy her curiosity. This sin will lead to consequences far beyond expected later in the story. Laris asks for a potion to turn things into gold. He is granted the vial but with a warning that gold is not in his destiny.

A few days later, deep in the forest, Roni and her friends are healing a blind man, which is witnessed by an ogre Bomo. The son of a powerful sorceress, he dabbles in spells and is successful only when luck is on his side. A woodcutter by profession, his lust for gold supersedes every other desire. He follows Roni and her friends, hoping to steal her away and make her his captive, and is extremely enraged when they disappear.

A second hunt organized by Eyvind brings the Imen back in time to save a hunted deer. Eyvind asks for the Imen's name and is granted his wish. Roni. But this time, there is another hiding in the shadows who craves Roni with the same fervor. Bomo wants to catch her unawares and make her his captive. But she vanishes just like before. He is caught spying by Eyvind and his friends but is let go.

In the city of Jasper, the capital city of Carron, Laris decides to sneak out into the forest and use the vial to turn things into gold. He goes into a cave to test the vial but is observed by Bomo who, in his lust for possessing all things gold, wants the vial. In the fight that occurs, the vial explodes into droplets, where each droplet turns everything into gold. In a fit of anger at losing this vial, Bomo takes Lari's sword and drives it deep into him, watching life depart from Lari's body as blood pools around him.

Meanwhile, in the city of Jasper, the wedding of Eyvind with Adina, the daughter of the rival kingdom Carthinia is announced in an attempt to bring peace to both kingdoms. But Eyvind is worried since Laris is nowhere to be found. He wants to go in search of him, but due to his responsibilities, sends Axel and Raidon.

They track deep into the forest where they find the body of their friend Laris. All of them are stunned and defeated. They are sure this is the work of the fiend Bomo about whom Raidon has always been suspicious. To pay their respect to their friend, they decide to take Laris back to Jasper to prepare for his funeral and return promptly after the ceremonies to apprehend Bomo.

And so there they are Bitten by greed for power and gold that will make them more Ruthless than ever before.

CRACK!

The furious whip-cracks on a lumbering beast echoed through the forest as Bomo hurried, his crude cart splintering branches while leaving devastation in its wake. He was in desperate haste to reach home, aware that if he were caught, he would be hung for killing an Imperial Knight.

Nothing mattered to him more than his greed and lust for gold. The glitter of the metal was his trigger, where even the surfeit amount he had amassed at home failed to satiate his avarice for it.

And there was Roni, the only creature who could match his desire for gold. She held the key to both his longings.

He had to make haste if he wanted to escape the Knights. Due to some strange luck, he had, so far, managed to get away from the elite soldiers; however, his mind rebuked him for letting a hoard of gold slip away from his hands.

He was furious and needed to find an outlet for the rage building in him. Several times, he thought about turning around to search for the man with the urn full of gold. But instincts told him that getting home was the safest way to stay alive.

The bumbling ogre made his way through the rough terrain and concealed paths since he chose not to take the oft-tread road.

Roni… Roni… Roni…

A name that never left his mind. A fervent prayer on his lips. He called out to her over and over. An obsession unbound growing within him. He had to find and trap her so that she was all his forever.

Besides, the maniacal ogre needed to make up for the gold that was lost to him and fretted to capture her. Only she could give him all the precious metal he could ever want in his life. And more.

But 'ow to capture her and make her mine?

He couldn't do this with the spells he knew now. He needed to search and get his hands on the books left by his mother and find the special one that would deliver her into his hands. And keep her chained to him forever.

Bomo thought hard about all the hidden places in his hovel and the specific book that he had to search to get to that specific spell.

Where cud mother 'ave 'idden it?

Frustrated by the slow pace they were traveling, he lashed out at the beast that seemed unaffected by the pelting of the whip. The ancient ox ignored his master and plodded wearily down the path. Bomo wanted to curse at the animal at the top of his lungs, but better sense prevailed at the last minute. And he realized that discretion was better. Making known his position to the Imperial Knights would only lead him to forsake his life.

The giant got down and rushed ahead, pulling at the reins to motivate the ox, but nothing worked. Eventually, Bomo gave in and waited with restless ardor until he reached his dwelling. He climbed off his cart and rushed toward the doorway. But suddenly he turned direction and ran around to the back of his house where he had tied Laris' horse.

He unhooked the reins, gave the horse a slap on its rump, and set it free into the forest, watching the animal disappear into the thicket until he knew it wouldn't come back to him.

A huge relief. He had, at last, gotten rid of the obvious evidence. Unbeknownst to him, this ogre didn't even think of looking down, where the ground was rife with hoof prints bearing the royal seal.

He gave one last look at the woods that were now still, then burst through the door of his home and bolted it securely behind him. Pressing his back against the wooden frame, he panted hard for a few minutes before rushing off to drag the heavy pieces of furniture and piled them against the back of the door, warding it from intruders. He gave the door a pull to check its strength, and satisfied with the barricade, he rushed through the cold hallway to his study.

Locking himself in, he ripped volumes of books off dusty shelves impatiently and threw them into a pile, his eyes glowing fiercely and his visage steeled with determination. His thick, calloused fingers flipped through the pages, tearing some of them in his haste, frantically searching for a spell. He knew the routine ones that his mother practiced would not help. It had to be the exact spell with precise words that would deliver Roni to his grubby clutches.

As time passed, the books were discarded one by one until the floor was laden with stacks of dusty volumes, thrown in a haphazard manner, with the impatient ogre sitting in the midst of them, searching for *the* spell. His crazed fervor increased with every book that did not reveal the secret, causing him to let out a loud growl of frustration followed by incomprehensible sounds. Bomo had reached a point of utter defeat when he suddenly noticed a glint from behind a dusty box that sat on one of the high shelves.

His gaping mouth spewed a screeching noise of delight as his attention was drawn toward that item. He wondered how long the object had been sitting there and how it had escaped his notice until now.

Wot could it be?

The clumsy creature rose to his feet, crossed over to the shelf and got on his tippy toes to reach for it. Only the tips of his thick fingers scraped against the item, evading the firmer grasp he was hoping for. He continued to stretch his bulky body, the promise of Roni motivating him. He looked around, wishing for a low stool to help him, but finding none, he kept trying until his endurance reached break point.

He mustered as much of his patience as he could, and eventually, by constantly clutching at it, he inched it closer to the edge. With one final swoop, he pulled it off the shelf and waited for it to fall into his graceless arms. It all happened in slow motion. Bomo watched the object come into view and slowly fall into his waiting arms, then slide past, almost dropping to the floor. Only a quick swerve managed to save the treasured book as he caught it just in time and held it close to his chest, now refusing to let it go.

This sudden maneuver caused him to lose his balance and fall backward on the ground over his discarded volumes. And he remained there, out of breath, clinging to the precious book and panting like the monster he was.

It took a moment or two to put right his breaths until his curiosity got the better of him as he slowly withdrew the object away from his chest to get a closer look.

His hands beheld an ancient tome, The Book of Spells — the title etched in gold. A leather buckle fastened the front cover to the back. Bomo drew the book close to his face as he read and reread the title in complete disbelief.

"I...I can't believe this. I can't..." he mumbled to himself over and over as he examined the book minutely taking in every stroke and texture. "The...Book...Of...Spells..." His voice quivered in awe and disbelief. He rolled over, crushing every other book under his bulk, and sat up.

It wasn't long before he unbuckled the book and tore open the pages to search for the spell he most longed for. The spell that would bind Roni to him.

Wot luck. Mine.

His face emanated a sudden glee as he studied the pages in disbelief. He remained seated on the floor, rifling through the pages, completely hypnotized by the spells that were within his reach to cast on others.

"I've noffing to fear now. I can turn any one of 'em into anyfing I like," he whispered, his confidence growing in leaps and bounds. Fate had finally dealt him a card of victory.

"Now I'll 'ave 'er for sure an' those who stand in me way best be wary 'cos I'll cast 'em into darkness!" he yelled out in arrogance.

"Why didn't she tell me about this book?" This annoyed him to no end as he cursed her long and hard into the afterlife.

The ogre continued searching through the book, looking for the exact spell needed for the task.

Hmmm, this one will work. He thought as he read through a spell.

Just when he thought he found the right spell, he found another that seemed more befitting than the previous. This went on for a while until he was in a state of complete confusion.

They all sounded good. There were spells that could turn a person into a statue or an animal or banish someone into darkness, along with a variety of other different outcomes. This was a book of dark possibilities.

The ogre contemplated each and every one of them, and just when he thought he found the perfect one, he realized that the list of ingredients needed for it was extensive and extremely difficult to obtain. At the moment, he didn't have much time to procure them. He shook his head in disapproval and wondered what to do next.

Maybe I should just keep it simple. Shrink 'er an' put 'er in a jar. He thought to himself about the various stuff he could try.

But wot if she dies? His brain rebutted.

The to-and-fro arguments went on forever. The more he thought about it, the more confused he became. *If only I could make a decision.*

He flipped back to the beginning of the book and perused through it carefully, reading even the footnotes until he noticed an odd word. At first, he made jest of it and believed the spell to be a prank.

The spell was titled "Cailloux," meaning pebbles.

"Turn 'er into pebbles? Wot good is that?" he asked himself as his lips twisted into a smirk.

Bomo laughed out loud at the very thought of turning anything into a pebble until the tiny half-working cell in his cranium yelled out.

Halt, you imbecile!

To which the specimen ceased his fit of laughter and let the brain reason with him.

If you turn 'er into a cailloux, you could 'ave possession of 'er FOREVER an' no one would ever know it 'cos she would be just a pebble, a cailloux. You could turn 'er into a pebble at any time, Bomo!

You could keep 'er close to your 'eart. She'd be yours forever.

The ogre scraped himself off the floor and rushed to his desk to examine the spell with more thoroughness under the flickering light of a candle.

He eagerly brought the flame closer to the pages, taking care to not set the book ablaze, flipped through the pages until he found the words of the spell and read it over and over several times, each time his mind assuring him this was the one.

He then flipped to the page that contained the list of ingredients needed to carry it out.

"Alabaster…? A Lightnin' rose? — Them roses are rare. Besides, those are 'ard to find most of the times anyhow. Now let's see… thistle, a 'eart of an unwounded creature…" He went on mumbling to himself as he thought about how he would acquire all these items.

But his heart sang in joy.

Yes, a pebble! I could 'ave 'er in me 'ands an' carry 'er with me all the time — no one would ever know. When I need 'er to make gold, I could change 'er back to Roni an' back again when I'm done. I will own 'er. Yes, indeed, I will own 'er. He sighed in contentment on finding such a brilliant plan.

His eyes burned feverishly as his thoughts overpowered him. He was completely delighted with his masterful scheme, nodding his giant head in approval.

With haste, he began the zealous search for all the necessary ingredients. Cupboards and shelves were rummaged to gather all the required items to conjure the spell. At long last, when the room was in shambles with every single thing upturned, he found the last item and decided to check the list in the book.

The golden book was nestled under his arm throughout his search and tightly held against his body. The ogre sat on the floor and opened the book to the "Cailloux" spell and went over the list once again. He didn't want to miss a single item, lest the spell failed, and he had to stop midway.

On careful scrutiny, it seemed he had all the ingredients, except for the Lightning rose, the alabaster, and the beating heart of an unwounded creature.

Three missin' 'fings. He repeated them in his head to remember. Now he had to leave his home to procure all of them.

The heart and the alabaster won't be difficult. However, the Lightning rose posed a problem. This mythical rose was rare and found only on the darkest moonless nights.

In the pitch-black night, its petals flashed a bluish-white light through its tiny veins, which made the whole flower glow to attract another creature, the Gia bug that helped pollinate it.

The Gia bugs were also rare, and that in itself hampered the pollination process, often leaving it unaccomplished.

One would think there had to be other creatures that aided in carrying the pollen of these glorious flowers. And it was true there were many that had attempted this. However, all of them had met with swift death the moment their tiny, fragile limbs touched the petals of the flower as they were electrified to death. The flower was that dangerous.

Only the Gia bug was resistant to the current that flowed through the veins of the Lightning rose, having insulated pads on its limbs that prevented the deadly shock. A Lightning rose in full bloom was a rare sight to see.

Bomo pressed his thick, hairy ear to the door of his study to listen for intruders on the other side, but he was met with silence. So, he cautiously cleared the barricade and entered the adjacent room. He repeated his actions at the front door, but before he opened it, he searched around the room for something to disguise himself. He found a large blanket that he threw over his bulky body and hunched his spine, deliberately making himself resemble an old woman.

With a sudden, silent twist of the knob, he threw the door open and waited awhile for a hint of movement around his home. He was met with silence, with only the routine nocturnal sounds reaching his ears. After a few moments, he realized there was no one lying in ambush for him, so he rushed out into the forest.

He stayed hidden in the shadows provided by the trees until he reached a clearing where he looked up at the sky to see if the moon was out. Unfortunately, for him, the sky was blanketed in clouds, and the ogre was unable to tell if it was a moonless night.

Bomo became frustrated and kicked the ground hard. He had a clear vantage point and didn't want to leave the area. He found a rock to perch upon to keep a watch on the skies. It would have been apparent to anyone that it was a pitch-black night when the clouds parted and yet the moon did not make an appearance. But Bomo lacked the common sense needed to observe the obvious.

He remained seated on the rock for several hours until finally, he took notice of the sky and saw the clouds had completely disappeared.

He stumbled around, staring up at the heavens, searching for the moon until the truth hit him on the head. It was indeed a moonless night. The creature, despite his huge bulk, could not contain his joy and jumped up and down. Now all he had to do was to find the rare flower. He quickly took to the deeper parts of the forest in search of the precious ingredient, investigating the slopes and hidden recesses. He even climbed up a dangerous precipice and hung over the edge to see if the rose grew on the underside. Such was his desperation.

He spent the better part of the night in search of this rose. The fear of being spotted and caught was bypassed by the desperate need to find this flower. He forgot about the Knights, even the one he had slain.

Now he was focused on his lust for gold and Roni, coveting both with obsessive persistence. The rusty gears in his brain churned and shook as he went over his master plan, salivating at the thought of capturing Roni and turning her into a *cailloux*.

He had already made plans to keep her in his shirt pocket, close to his heart, and whenever he needed something, he would change her back and compel her to grant him his wishes. Chambers of gold, so much that every urn would overflow, where he could sit in gold and sleep on it if he so wished. All of which Roni would help acquire. His lust grew in leaps and bounds with each passing moment.

"If she could grant gold to a greedy-no-good-peasant like the blind man, then surely she would grant me a wish. After all, I'm a 'ard workin' man an' far more 'andsome than 'im. If only I 'adn't stopped to eat, I could've easily snapped 'is neck an' been off with the gold," he cursed himself.

It was getting late in the night, and dawn was only a few hours away, yet there was no sign of sleep in Bomo's eyes. The creaky brain inside his huge cranium worked so hard to help him think where he could find the rose that he hadn't yawned a single time the entire night. His obsession to find the ingredient before the night ended reached a zenith that he now began to see things. He saw flashes in distant shrubs only to discover they were nothing more than ordinary flowers. Sometimes there was really nothing there.

In a fit of rage, he began to rip out vegetation from the ground and tossed them about. Once he even picked up a large rock to smash the plants he had insanely torn out from the ground. Stumbling through the forest in complete frustration, he reached the point of giving up entirely.

RONI WAS IN THE middle of her final rehearsal with Suki when she felt a sharp force hit her in the gut. Something had occurred in the forest, and the signal was extremely strong.

She looked at Suki and Kenji—they appeared to be not affected by it at all.

"Didn't you feel that?" she asked them.

"Feel what?" they both asked simultaneously.

"That siren. It was so strong and strange," she replied with a confused look on her face.

They both gave her a puzzled look, not knowing what she was talking about.

"The siren," she repeated, pointing up. "You didn't feel that?"

"No," replied Kenji. Worry crossed his eyes as he focused his gaze on her. There was something definitely wrong with Roni, and he was determined to get to the bottom of it.

Looking at both their expressions, Roni started doubting herself. *Did I really feel it? Or is it the same nagging feeling in my gut that I have been getting since the time I met Eyvind?*

But this felt so different from the last time. She couldn't put her finger on it. Unable to resolve what it was or where it originated from, she decided to get on with the rehearsal and waste no time thinking about it. She could deal with whatever came her way later. But the thought remained in her mind, and all she wanted was the strange feeling to simply go away. She wanted everything to go back to the way it used to be. She picked up the dandum sticks and began to go through the movements halfheartedly. Distracted and bothered by not being able to explain what the siren was, especially since the others had not heard it, her movements were clumsy and awkward.

"Roni. Pay attention," yelled out Kenji.

The rehearsal once again came to a halt, and she stood still, dropping her head into her hands with the dandum sticks tucked under her arm. She rubbed her face with her palms, hoping she could snap out of whatever was ailing her.

"Are you all right?" asked Suki as she approached her friend and stood before her.

"Yes, I think I am," Roni replied without certainty.

"You seem distracted. Would you like to stop and resume later?" she asked.

Roni agreed. It would give her time to collect herself and resolve what troubled her.

Again, she wondered if it had anything to do with the strange nagging sensation she had been feeling since her encounter with Eyvind. But this one was very different.

The force continued to impinge upon her, and yet it didn't seem to affect anyone else. It all seemed very weird.

Roni dropped the dandum sticks and hurried out of the auditorium, leaving Kenji and Suki behind, stunned. They called out to her several times, but she had no answer to give them. What could she explain when she didn't know it herself?

She waved her hand in the air in acknowledgment of their words and rushed out.

"Who'd know the answer to this?" she muttered to herself.

She thought hard about whom she should go to.

Maybe I should ask Father? She wondered about her options. *Perhaps not... The high priestess!* She exclaimed to herself in satisfaction.

Roni ran toward the temple, hurrying past people as fast as she could. Moments later, she arrived at a large, circular, dome-shaped structure located at the center of Imen-Hera.

She felt its soothing force nourish her from head to toe.

Roni hurried up the steps, and then down one of eight radiating isles until she arrived at the raised circular altar upon which stood the high priestess engaged in her daily duties.

It was here that all ceremonies in Imen-Hera were conducted, their most sacred inner sanctum.

Roni approached the altar and noticed the eight lower priests standing equidistant from one another, encircling the raised altar. They remained motionless and focused while awaiting instructions from the high priestess, Miwa.

A mature but gracile woman, she stood tall, devoid of emotion, while engaged in her daily duties. She was clad in a ceremonial white gown that was clinched in the back and wrapped at the front.

Roni stood at the edge of the altar, silent, waiting for the priestess to notice her. And she didn't have to wait long. Her painful, tortured face and restless demeanor interrupted Miwa's focus.

The priestess slowly opened her eyes to see who it was but remained expressionless. She proceeded with her duties until she was done and then motioned Roni to approach the altar.

Roni nervously stepped up and stood before her. Slightly taller than Roni, Miwa had an aura giving her a presence making her larger than life. The knot in Roni's stomach tightened, and a burning sensation rose up into her chest.

Miwa maintained her silence and studied the young girl with penetrating eyes. Moments lapsed and then she gestured to one of the priests on the periphery who immediately came to life from his statuesque state and disappeared behind a door.

He returned moments later with a large golden hoop and a smoking censer. The hoop had eight knots tied equidistant from one another. The priest approached the altar with his head bowed low and handed both items to Miwa. He then returned to his earlier sentinel position.

Fear of having her secret revealed to Miwa consumed Roni. She realized she had been poisoned thoroughly, as she had coveted Eyvind's world as well as Eyvind himself. She wondered if Miwa could read her mind and her secret desires.

The high priestess did not utter a single word, which made Roni even more nervous and uneasy. She couldn't even guess how much Miwa knew.

In the midst of her inner turmoil, Roni forgot the priestess possessed the power to see anything withheld from her, and the moment she made eye contact with Roni, she was able to see everything that ailed her.

Miwa pointed to the center of the altar as Roni stepped forth and occupied the spot. Handing the smoking censer to Roni, Miwa raised the golden loop above Roni's head, encircling her body, then lowered it gently to the floor as she recited an ancient chant silently.

Roni was motioned to step out of the hoop as Miwa took the censer and placed it in the center of the hoop.

At first, small wisps of smoke emerged from the ornate vents, but soon thick smoke began to bellow out and take form.

Roni stared in horror at the smoky shape. She leaned forward to get a closer look, while Miwa continued to watch Roni with penetrating eyes.

The smoke took the shape of a man who lay fallen on the ground as Roni then felt a sharp pain in her chest that brought her to her knees. She stared in terror.

The man lay prone on the ground — Roni was unable to see his face. She was familiar with the man's regalia, which horrified her.

Could it be Eyvind? Her heart beat faster even at the mere thought of it.

She walked around the spectral form and looked at it from all directions, trying hard to catch a glimpse of the face.

Miwa continued to observe Roni in silence, not a single flicker of expression on her face. Her entire mien remained unaffected and stoic.

Anxiety seized Roni as she became feverishly impatient to find out who it was. Blood rushed into her ears as her pulse raced, and her fingers trembled as she reached into the smoke to see if she could turn the spectral body over to have a better look. She looked back at Miwa as she was doing so to make sure she was not about to do anything forbidden.

Miwa remained still, giving no indication of disapproval, so Roni proceeded.

The smoke was dense, as if had a life of its own. Roni could feel the thickness of this mass clamping around her wrist as she clenched her teeth tightly and gently rolled the spectral form over. The moment she laid her eyes upon the man, she let out a sigh of relief and staggered a few steps back, falling onto the floor.

It's not him. It's not him. It's not him.

She repeated the words in her head in relief as her heart began slowing down. She could at last take a full breath.

Miwa, however, was unmoved by the events that were transpiring before her. Her gaze remained focused on Roni.

Tears streamed down Roni's face as she sat on the floor in a heap. The knot in her stomach loosened, but the strange feelings, never felt before, ravaged her insides. She couldn't understand what it was or the reason she felt the way she did.

What's happening to me? What is this weird emotion I am feeling? Why is water pouring out of my eyes?

She wiped the tears from her face and stared at her wet hands in shock. She had never wept before. She looked around to find the cause of it. The censer was now hardly producing any more smoke. So, it was not due to the fumes.

Roni rose to her feet and faced the priestess, uncertain of what Miwa would say. There was no response other than her silent, penetrating stare.

Miwa knew what Roni was hiding. Roni dropped to her knees in front of her and begged for clemency.

"I know I disobeyed the sacred law, but I didn't mean to. It wasn't my intention. I'm not sure what came over me. Curiosity, perhaps?" she whimpered.

Miwa was unaffected by Roni's emotions, who continued to struggle with grief and shame.

Finally, the High Priestess spoke, "As you know, curiosity leads one down dangerous paths and forbidden recesses from where there's no way back."

Roni was speechless and didn't have a reply, knowing she couldn't deny the truth or Miwa's assessment. She had failed her people.

She was too embarrassed to look at Miwa, so she nodded in agreement, staying where she was, with her eyes cast down and head bowed.

She awaited her sentence, but Miwa said nothing.

"I'll accept any punishment," Roni at last stated as she wiped the tears from her face.

Miwa motioned her to rise to her feet and started speaking when Roni stood before her, uncertainty written across her features about the consequences she would now have to bear. "Your punishment has already been dealt to you. You'll forever feel grief and sorrow from which you once had immunity. Nothing can be a worse punishment for an Imen. Don't you agree?" she asked.

Roni nodded as she experienced the true gravity of the results of her action. She had breached the sacred law, and now she was alone in this punishment.

"An inevitable transformation is upon you, one that you cannot avert or escape. It is the reason why this law is the most sacred. Do you understand?" Miwa paused, waiting for a visual confirmation.

Roni nodded and felt numb as she realized the true seriousness of her deed. A feeling of immense dread assailed her as if the ground below had opened up.

"You have delved into reigns far beyond what is allowed. Curiosity has a powerful hypnotic lure that draws one to covet things, especially those outside of Imen-Hera," she continued her grave lecture. "Your glow will soon fade, and you'll no longer be one of us. You'll be banished from Imen-Hera…forever."

With that, Miwa departed the altar, leaving Roni to face her newly acquired demon all by herself.

Roni looked around and saw that the remaining eight priests remained statuesque in their original positions.

She looked up at the enormous crystal that projected down from the ceiling onto the center of the altar like a giant stalactite. Even this powerful crystal couldn't erase what she had done.

Distraught, she stepped off the altar to make her way back to the amphitheater. She felt her light fading with every step. Profound emptiness opened up inside her, threatening to swallow her whole. The weight of what she had done bore down heavily upon her. She thought about her parents and wondered how she would explain everything to them.

The uncomfortable changes impinged upon her, and with no understanding of what she should do, she fought hard to hold it all in. She felt sad, alone, and scared. The Imen were impervious to such emotions. But she now had to bear the brunt of it all.

As she walked, Miwa's words echoed in her head. Fear wrapped its tendrils around her before she could finish her thought. Only one question echoed in her mind.

Where would she go when the transformation was complete?

Eventually, even the Boad trees would not allow her entry back into Imen-Hera.

A weight of despair crushed her as her spirits sank. Each step was a reminder of what was yet to come. And with each step, her transformation progressed, writing her future in stone.

THE LAST LIGHT OF the day retracted from the forest after having cast long, crisp shadows which now blurred and faded fast, giving way to darkness. The wind whistled through the trees that stood tall like the unwavering sentinels they were, weathering time day in and day out.

Raidon noticed the fast-creeping shadows that enveloped them and made the decision to set up camp and rest for the night. Axel and Raidon carefully wrapped their cloaks around Laris' body and laid him gently to rest upon a large, flat white alabaster rock. These rocks dotted the entire forest and were a source of light for the land of Imen-Hera, unbeknownst to those dwelling above.

Axel scouted around their campsite to patrol the perimeter and ensure their safety when he noticed a rare sight. Secretly growing among thick shrubs was a single glowing rose.

"Raidon, come here. Quick!"

"What is it?" asked Raidon as he hurried over.

"Look!" He pointed to the rose, his voice filling with awe

Raidon's eyes widened in joy as he took in the wondrous sight. "It's a Lightning rose," he whispered as he crouched down to have a closer look at it.

"A what?" Axel inched closer and bent down. He wanted to capture every single detail of this rare flower, sparkling in its glory, forever in his mind.

"A Lightning Rose. It's a rare flower. This is a true wonder before our eyes," Raidon remarked in complete amazement.

Both their gazes were transfixed on the flower that fluoresced with its bluish-white light. Seeing the two men whispering in hushed tones, the others too approached closer to see what they were looking at.

"What is it?" asked one of the guards quietly.

"A Lightning Rose," whispered Axel.

"A what?" asked the guard, hunching over to take a closer look.

The flower caused all the toughened soldiers to lower their voices, knowing that this was a sight they would never see again perhaps in their lifetimes. So awestruck were they by this image.

Everyone joined Raidon and Axel, wanting to know more.

"Does it have a scent?" asked one of the guards as he stretched his neck forward to sniff the air.

"It doesn't," replied Raidon, then stretched a hand into the shrubs and plucked the gem off the tiny bush, much to everyone's shock. The flower didn't have enough current to affect Raidon, other than a slight sting on the initial touch. The others were astounded to witness such an action.

"What're you going to do with it?" asked Axel.

Raidon's eyes remained fixed on the flower, and although he heard the question, he continued to rotate the stem slowly with his fingers to soak in its beauty.

All the men now surrounded him, their faces drawing closer to the flower.

"It's a holy flower used in sacred ceremonies by high priests. So rare, yet here it is in my hands," stated Raidon.

"How fortunate. We've seen things lately that most people couldn't possibly have, less imagined, in several lifetimes. And now we have this Lightning Rose," Raidon continued as he stepped back and faced Laris' lifeless body, which lay motionless upon the white rock.

He walked toward it and placed the rose on Laris' chest. Within moments, the alabaster rock upon which Laris was laid out glowed brightly. It was a magical radiance. A hushed silence fell upon this group of men.

The Imperial Knights stood back and watched this fantastic sight.

"Is it going to bring him back to life?" asked one of the guards.

"Who knows? But I don't think so. Unfortunately, he's long departed and passed on. We can only honor him with this gesture," replied Raidon in a melancholic tone.

They respectfully bowed their heads low and eventually dispersed to bed down for the night.

In the stillness of the air around this part of the forest, the dark corpse remained upon the glowing rock while the Knights took shifts to keep watch throughout the night.

BOMO GAVE UP LOOKING for the Lightning Rose and began to make his way back to his lair to retire for the rest of the night when something caught his eye.

He lumbered in its direction and drew closer but became frightened by the shadowy figures moving around a glowing object.

"Wot's that?" he asked himself.

He remained where he was and tried to make sense of what his simple brain was showing him. Upon closer examination, he noticed that the dark figures were horses tied to a tree; however, he couldn't make out the glow.

Now that he had established the moving figures were not specters, he began to inch closer to get a better look, taking one careful stride at a time to avoid stepping on crackling twigs.

But he forgot he was built like a giant and possessed as much grace as a lumbering ox. His stealth was a thing of his imagination. He bumbled in the direction of the horses that were tied to the left of the glow. And in his eagerness, he stepped on a large rock and lost his footing, causing him to fall and make a loud ruckus. He remained seated on the ground as he whispered curses at the rock.

Moments later, he saw a shadowy figure move about in the darkness with a loaded bow. Bomo crouched down and lay flat on the forest floor, trying to remain as motionless as he could. But this was a Knight whom he had rattled with his noise, and the soldier was never going to leave this alone.

The Knight was alerted by the strange sound and moved in its direction to investigate. The arrow stayed nocked in the bow as he parted the darkness with its tip.

Bomo made a clumsy attempt to peek up and find out where the guard was. To his dismay, the Knight was just a few feet away and familiar to him. He was the same who had interrupted his transaction earlier that day.

The ogre's pulse raced, and his heart pounded hard, wanting to escape the confines of his rib cage. He was sure he would be caught. No sooner had he looked at the soldier than he plopped back down on the forest floor, struggling to remain motionless, despite his slipping ability to control the fear and anxiety that consumed him.

The guard was quick on his feet and as silent as an assassin. He moved about with weightless speed and agility while maintaining his cover. He was within a couple of feet of Bomo when he heard a voice. The guard turned around and waved his hand in the air, giving his response.

Bomo struggled to stay still, not moving an inch. By now, fear had gripped his throat as if his life was being choked out of him. His mind started playing tricks, and he began imagining the things that would happen to him as soon as the Knights discovered him. His eyes turned red, and his breaths stopped. He clutched his chest tightly as his heart pounded harder against his breastbone with each pulse.

Soon there were two guards in his proximity, and although he was unable to see what they were doing, he could tell they were in silent communication with one another.

The ogre felt the sword of the inevitable. He could feel the steel blade run through his chest and put an end to his miserable life.

His gold hoard, the fruit of his hard labor, flashed before his yellowish-red eyes. The murder of the Imperial Knight also thundered in his dense cranium. He knew it was certain death once they set their eyes upon him. The ogre lay trembling on the ground in bouts of fear until a sound came from the opposite direction. A rustling of bushes and the guards pounced into action. They both ran in opposite directions to encircle the area.

Bomo maintained his position of hiding for a moment until he could fully ascertain the guards had left. He slowly lifted his massive cranium to take a peek at them as well as figure out a way to leave this place. He saw their silhouettes move at a distance in the opposite direction and seized the moment to make his getaway.

His heart raced even faster as he got up and started to run, looking over his shoulder to make sure the guards had not spotted him. However, the strange glow caught his eye and made him halt on the spot. Seeing none of the Knights around him raised his confidence and soothed his anxiety considerably.

Curiosity caught hold of him, and he knew he couldn't possibly leave without seeing what it was exactly. He searched around to find a vantage point to have a better look without having to go back. He looked up at the trees and thought about climbing one. He reached for one of the branches within his grasp, and just as he put all his weight on the limb to give him leverage, he heard it crack, which echoed throughout the forest.

He immediately released his grip and hid behind some shrubs, ducking low. Bomo cursed the tree limb and himself over and over in frustration. He pounded the air with his tightly clenched fists. He waited for the pounding of feet and the whispers of the Knights drawing in on him. After a while, he realized that the sound of the branch hadn't been loud enough to warrant anyone's attention. His yellow eyes peered up from behind the shrubs as he looked around to make sure the coast was clear before emerging from his hiding place once again.

Luckily, the guards were not alerted to the rustling of leaves and stayed off in the distance. The night sounds in the forest were too many for them to go chasing after each one.

Bomo bent as low as his spine would allow and crept in the direction of the camp toward the glow. Finally, though a little further from where he would like to be, he was in a position to get a decent look. He could roughly make out what he was seeing— a body wrapped in a cloak resting on a softly glowing large white rock — and then his eyes narrowed in on the magnificently electrified Lightning Rose. He fell back in shock the moment his gaze landed upon it.

It can't be! Is it really...? He wondered in complete disbelief.

At first, he thought his eyes were playing tricks on him. He had spent the entire evening staring hard at things that appeared to be the Lightning Rose, but sadly enough, all of them turned out to be nothing.

The ogre sat up once again and rubbed his eyes with his rough, calloused knuckles and looked at the rose once again. No. No tricks. It really was the Lightning Rose. The creature was beside himself.

Wot luck! He rejoiced and announced this finding to his brain. He could not believe his success.

Now, there was only one question that remained in his tiny simple brain.

How was he going to get it away from them?

The guard was much too close for him to make a bold move, so Bomo decided to wait for a more opportune moment.

THE GUARD ON WATCH heard an odd noise and carefully moved in its direction while remaining alert enough to not wander too far from his post.

He looked around in the dark but saw nothing. Another guard joined him, and moments later, they both heard a strange noise from the opposite direction. They inched closer to the area and upon rounding the source, they noticed it was just a deer.

Putting away their bows, they returned to their camp where they kept a vigilant watch.

The night was alive with a symphony of wild noises, each creature singing its own song, yet there was a rhythm to it. The clouds had long passed leaving in their wake a dark sky glittering with millions of stars.

Beneath the canopy of stars lay a fallen knight upon a glowing rock — truly somber but a magnificent sight, nonetheless. The stars slowly arced across the sky as the night progressed, bringing with it the native sonata of sounds.

As daylight drew closer, the sounds of hoots and screeches, buzzes and hums gave way to chirps and songs of the morning birds, the buzzing of the bees, and other small creatures that signaled the beginning of a new day. At the horizon, daylight slowly bleached the dark sky, showcasing a canvas of pink and orange strokes of the rising sun.

Dawn arrived, and a thick blanket of fog descended upon the forest floor. The rock on which Laris was laid pierced the fog like an island surrounded by the moving wisps of mist.

The Imperial Knights began to rise and emerge from the fog. They rubbed their eyes, dusted themselves off, and took swigs of water from their leather water bags.

"Strange night," remarked one of the guards.

"How so?" asked Raidon.

"Not sure. Strange noises and a feeling of being watched," he replied.

"I'm sure we were being watched by more than just one thing," Raidon replied, trying to make light of the situation.

"I don't know. It was eerie," the guard added as he looked around with an uneasy feeling.

"Shall we check it out?" asked Raidon.

"Wonder if it was the woodcutter? I'll spare him no mercy," ranted Axel.

"That's enough. You'll get your chance to bring him to justice. Right now, we have a bigger task to tend to," replied Raidon.

Axel looked around to see if the woodcutter was in sight as his jaw clenched in anger. There was no one there other than themselves.

They took one last look around, gathered everything, and prepared to leave.

The rock upon which Laris lay still glowed with the Lightning Rose on his chest.

The men gathered their belongings and loaded their horses, but just as they were about to pick Laris up, they heard the sound of an approaching horse. They reached for their swords and awaited its arrival.

Moments later, a jet-black horse without a rider emerged from the fog at the edge of the clearing. The men stood motionless for a moment staring at the stallion. It looked familiar.

"Tohl? Is that Tohl?" yelled out Axel as he raced in the horse's direction.

The men watched him approach the scared horse.

The horse immediately recognized Axel and Raidon as it pranced towards them.

"It is Tohl!" exclaimed Axel, looking back at the rest of them.

Overjoyed, Axel caressed the magnificent animal while stroking its neck and back.

By now, others surrounded it as Raidon stroked the stallion's head and smiled in delight. They examined the horse, carefully making sure it was not injured. No wounds on it. It was just dirty.

"You're filthy, Tohl. Look at you. What've you been up to?" mocked Axel.

The men led the horse close to their camp, and as Tohl set eyes upon his master's body, he hung his head low and gracefully walked up to Laris.

He looked at him, head to toe, as if expecting Laris to get up and carry on as they had for years. However, there was no response. Tohl's eyes filled with tears. It was evident he knew but was not ready to let go.

He stepped forward and nudged the cold, lifeless body with his nose, but there was still no response. The horse continued to nudge him several times as silent tears streamed down his long black nose.

The men stood by in dignified silence, watching the painful scene. The bond between the horse and his master and the loss of it affected them all.

Raidon walked up to Tohl and tried to console him. He stroked Tohl's neck and back, reassuring him in a soft tone, barely audible to the rest.

Tohl got up on his hind legs and kicked his forelegs wildly.

Raidon ducked to avoid being kicked, but he knew the horse would not intentionally harm him.

Eventually, Tohl came to grips that his master was gone, and his final duty was to carry the broken body back home.

The men draped Laris' body across Tohl's back and covered it with a cloak, securing it for the ride.

Raidon took the Lightning Rose and tucked it in the harness.

The soldiers took one last look around and mounted their horses. In a single file, they cut their way through the early morning fog to travel back to Jasper.

BOMO SPENT THE NIGHT restlessly scurrying the forest floor but stayed close to the Imperial Knights' camp. He was overwhelmed and frustrated with his failure to acquire what he coveted the most, especially since it was within reach, yet so far away.

At times, he stretched his arm out into the darkness and tried to grasp the Lightning Rose from a distance. The object of his desire was in the midst of danger, however much he wanted it to be within his grasp.

The creature became increasingly psychotic as he sat in the darkness, pretending to hold the rose in his hand and mentally going through the motions of adding it as the final ingredient to the potion he would brew for the Cailloux spell.

Bomo's imagination carried him away — at times, he really thought he was back at home, cooking the spell over the fire in his large black cauldron. He would waver back and forth from moments of lucidity to complete lunacy.

He spent most of the night crawling around on his fat belly, moving from one vantage point to another, trying to get a better and closer look at the rose, while figuring a way to evade the soldiers.

If only there wozn't so many of 'em. He cursed all of them in his mind while pounding his fists softly into the ground.

No matter what he tried, he couldn't come up with a plan to steal the rose. There were just too many soldiers.

Most of all, he feared losing his hoard buried back at home. Each time the spiteful creature peeked up to look at the magnificent flower, he was consumed with anger, and his innards writhed in torment. His intense need to get the flower burned him from the inside out.

Occasionally, he looked up at the night sky to gauge how much time he had left before dawn crept in.

Dense fog swept through the forest floor, and Bomo felt it might play in his favor. He thought about sneaking under its cover to pilfer what he wanted and slip away quietly.

The lumbering idiot lay on his belly and began to advance himself forward on his elbows and knees. Although he tried to be stealthy, he made enough noise to wake up the creatures a mile away.

He became very angry with himself for lacking the graceful agility to move quietly.

At one time, the guard on watch was spooked by Bomo's ruckus, and it was not long before another guard woke up to investigate. Bomo remained paralyzed, hugging the ground, hoping they would not discover him.

His own loud disturbance filled him with panic as he crawled back into the forest as fast as he could without drawing further attention to himself. Upon reaching a safe distance, he hid behind a large tree and peered from it. He watched the guard's every move.

Bomo tried to keep his eyes transfixed on the flower as if, in doing so, the rose would come to him. But staring at it hard made his eyes heavy with sleep as he began to fade. It wasn't long before he crumpled on the ground, and fell fast asleep like an overgrown grotesque baby.

Crisp rays of sunlight pierced the forest and stabbed Bomo's face. He woke up to the brilliant, blinding light.

For a moment, he thought he had succeeded in snatching the rose, and it was the brightness of the flower that had blinded him. It took a little while for the ogre to come to the sobering reality of realizing his hands were bare, and the bright light was the new day's sun.

He shot up, standing upright, and looked around for the guard as well as the precious Lighting Rose, but they had all vanished. Bomo was enraged. He restrained himself from yelling out loud in case the guards were still in the vicinity.

He had slept through everything.

The specimen made his way slowly to the rock upon which Laris' body had lain and searched for the rose everywhere, just in case the guard had discarded it.

His creepy yellow eyes combed the area as thoroughly as he could in hopes of finding it but to no avail.

Bomo fell to his knees, throwing his arms up in the air, arching his back and whispered curses at his mother for his bad luck.

THE LOW DENSE FOG parted to allow an enormous drum to emerge slowly in the backdrop of the soft melodic tune of the percussion instruments. Brightly dressed figures began to come into view and take shape as they encircled and arranged themselves around the drum. With colorful *dandum* sticks in their hands, they were poised in different stances to strike on cue. When the moment arrived, they hit the giant drum in synchronicity.

At first, a deep rumbling sound came from the belly of the drum soon building up to a thunderous roar. The dancers built up the momentum from the soft strikes to the harder ones, hitting it in unison until the beats reverberated in the entire room and then freezing with the sticks high above their heads, motionless. The silence was more melodious than the drums as it spoke of the scene about to unfurl in front of their eyes.

Then, a gentle stream of percussion music started playing in the background as the center of the drum, which was solid, opened slowly with Roni and Suki emerging from it. They took center stage while the others arranged themselves around the two girls. Then the dancers turned to one another and struck their *dandum* sticks, making an energetic sound.

Immediately Roni and Suki sprang into action. They twirled and swung the sticks against each other and then on the outer edge of the drum, where the membranous portion caused the rhythm to echo in sync with the audience's heartbeat. The strength in their postures and the grace in their movements resembled warriors engaged in a fierce fight to the death with one another. The audience was in awe at the magnificence of their flawless performance. The entire auditorium was filled with thunderous energy, making it difficult for anyone to remain motionless in their seats. It was indeed a spectacular sight.

Roni and Suki were agile performers, who showed off their dexterities in motions that seemed to defy nature's laws, never failing to strike the *dandum* sticks at the precise time.

Kenji was pleased with his composition, his face aglow with complete satisfaction, his music well complemented by the dancers.

The intensity of the performance built up high, exhausting every last ounce of energy from each dancer. Then came the thunderous conclusion which rose to a crescendo and ended with the performers frozen in time — a sight to see.

Loud applause broke out, and the ebullition of the crowd was uncontrollable.

The dancers remained motionless for a few breaths. Eventually, they came to life and took their bows. Seeing the audience's ovation, Suki was very pleased with herself and was glad Roni had talked her into performing with her. Wanting to share her joy with her best friend, she turned her head toward her and was shocked to see a pale Roni by her side. There were no signs of happiness radiating from her face.

Suki smiled politely at everyone who congratulated her and became self-conscious about her own performance and wondered if she had disappointed Roni in any way. Eventually, the applause died out, and the two girls vanished back into the drum.

"That was brilliant, wasn't it?" Suki commented energetically to Roni, trying to pep her up, as they stepped off the stage with confidence.

"Yes, it was," replied Roni, her voice low and rough with held-back tears, knowing this was the last time she would ever perform in Imen-Hera.

"You don't seem as pleased. Is everything all right? Did I do something wrong? I thought I was in step all the way," Suki asked her self-consciously, but her questions were immediately interrupted by a throng of people rushing to congratulate them.

They got lost in the shuffle and pulled away from each other before Roni had a chance to answer Suki.

Eventually, Roni worked herself away from the crowd and tried to look for Suki, but there was no sign of her. Retreating to her dressing room, she made the decision to let her parents and friends know what she had done and what lay ahead for her without further delay. But this was an uphill task. She tried to work out, in her mind, how she would break the news to them, especially to her parents. They would be devastated, completely heartbroken. She contemplated her fate and looked back at all the fun and good times she'd had over the many years.

Tears welled up in her eyes as she wondered how long it would be before she was denied entry back into Imen-Hera. Trembling with uncertainty, she examined her face and hands. Her heart shuddered when she noticed they looked dull. The change had begun, and soon everyone would know unless she told them first.

Her introspections were interrupted by a knock on the door. She quickly dried her eyes and got up to let her parents in, Emperor Mihara and Empress Kimiko. Her quaking legs could no longer support her, so she sat back uncomfortably in her chair.

Both parents approached her, beaming with pride, but looking at her pale face, they sensed something was amiss. There was no happiness shining from Roni.

Something was seriously wrong. Kimiko glanced at her husband, wondering if they should pry into Roni's matters. Mihara gave a quick shake of his head and congratulated his daughter for delivering a flawless and magnificent performance.

"That was marvelous! Well executed," he stated proudly.

"It most certainly was," agreed her mother with great pride and enthusiasm, taking her cue from her husband. She moved closer to caress Roni's face and gently hugged her, pressing her head against her bosom.

Roni leaned into her mother's embrace for a few seconds, then looked up to smile awkwardly at her, but added nothing. She knew if she opened her mouth, she would cry.

Her father stayed silent, giving Roni the opportunity to tell them what was bothering her, but no words were forthcoming. An awkward tension quickly rose in the air around them, bringing to mind a sense of impending doom. Their daughter had never been so quiet in her entire life.

Kimiko moved a step back, breaking the embrace, and then tilted up her daughter's chin to look into her face to understand what was ailing her. Roni certainly didn't look right.

Was it her makeup? The lights? No. She didn't think so.

Something else was eating Roni from the inside. The mother's heart started beating fiercely.

"What's the matter?" she asked tenderly, stroking her hair, as she had done when Roni was a child.

Roni remained silent, still debating whether she should confess her wretched fate to them. Finally, she concluded she didn't have much time. This was it. The dreaded moment had arrived when she would break their hearts.

She got up from the chair and turned to her father, then wrapped her arms tightly around his neck and wept silently. She just couldn't bring herself to tell them what she had done. Mihara felt his daughter's pain rip his insides but was puzzled about what could have caused her such anguish.

He felt her tears seeping through his clothes and knew this was not a typical behavior for an Imen. The Imen do not express such deep emotions, which concerned Mihara and Kimiko. Her father tenderly unwound Roni's hands from around his neck and stepped back to look at her.

Kimiko stepped closer and asked with grave concern, "You're crying. What's the matter, Roni?"

Standing before them with her tear-soaked face hanging low, Roni shook her head in complete disbelief at what she had done, although deep within, a small part of her felt no regret. It was as if it were meant to be.

"Roni! What's the matter?" demanded her mother as she gripped her by the shoulders. Looking at the stream of tears that ran down Roni's face, she asked fearfully, "Tears?"

Mihara quickly figured out what it might be, although he hoped it wasn't so. By now, Roni had begun sobbing hard.

"She's crying. Why is she crying? She doesn't look well," Kimiko commented to her husband.

She became increasingly worried, and somewhere in the depths of her, the answer stirred around in the darkest region of her mind. But she refused to acknowledge or give it any credence.

I won't allow such thoughts to enter my head, she thought to herself. She grabbed her daughter's hand and kissed it over and over, knowing she was about to lose her.

Roni couldn't bear to torture her parents with the uncertainty anymore.

She pulled her hand away to regain her composure and began, "I've failed you both. I violated our most sacred law. I have to leave Imen-Hera," she stated quietly as she raised her hands in front of her face and stared at them, back to front in complete disbelief.

"Look. The change has begun," she continued, holding back her tears and letting her hands fall helplessly to her side.

"What do you mean?" cried out her mother, refusing to accept the truth. She pushed the answer back into the deepest recess of her mind, but it continued to surge forth. "I won't hear it," she continued murmuring in shock, shaking her head as if she could ward off what was inevitable.

Roni couldn't bear to look at her distraught mother and hated herself for bringing them such pain. She was witnessing how a single selfish act could rip apart so many lives.

Mihara remained silent, but he too was devastated by Roni's confession.

How could this be? What could have driven her to break our most sacred law?

The same questions played on a loop in his mind. He opened his mouth to say something but found himself at a loss for words. For the first time in his life, he was speechless.

He held Roni by her shoulders and took a long look at his precious child and then pressed her tightly against his chest. He could feel her sob silently as her agony pierced him like a sharp knife, shredding anything in its way.

Kimiko stood by silently, suffering her own anguish.

Although it was impossible for people in Imen-Hera to cry, every Imen could feel pain and suffering when they came across a loss such as this. There was nothing they could do other than logically face the next step.

They had to prepare Roni for her departure because she would soon transform completely and be barred from entering back into Imen-Hera.

Kimiko spoke in a somber tone, "Come. We must prepare."

Roni lifted her face from her father's chest and wiped her tear-soaked face. Firming her shoulders, she nodded in agreement.

"But first, how long has this transformation been in progress?" asked her mother.

Roni's mind immediately transported her back to the moment when she first encountered the wounded hunter whom she had aided. Again, she was lost in the moment. Such was the pull that the human had on her.

Kimiko and Mihara watched Roni as she stared into space and relived the moment.

"Roni! How long has it been?" Kimiko shook her and repeated the question.

Roni snapped back into reality and began counting the days in her head.

"Maybe a few weeks, I think," she answered with uncertainty.

"A few weeks!" Kimiko was shocked. Both parents couldn't believe what they were hearing. It usually took less than a month before a transformation was complete.

How have we missed this? She may already be running out of time. Kimiko thought to herself in horror. "We must hurry," she instructed Mihara.

They escorted Roni to the royal quarters, evading passersby, who stopped to congratulate her on her outstanding performance. She politely accepted the praises and continued to hurry along.

Upon reaching her parent's quarters, her mother bolted the door shut for the very first time.

Ginji, one of their attendants, was summoned and instructed not to let anyone disturb them. He immediately complied and stood as a sentinel at the entrance.

Kimiko and Mihara faced their daughter and soaked in as much of her as they could. They knew they were losing her forever, but their minds couldn't fathom what led her to this, however much they wanted to understand her predicament.

But what was done was done, and it couldn't be changed. Thinking back in time, they remembered the moment when Miwa had warned them of the consequences of their asking her for a child. The penalty was to lose that child one day. However, over the years, they had refused to accept Miwa's words of caution and had tried to forget that day would ever arrive. Sadly for them, that day had now arrived.

They now had to focus on what needed to be done. They had to ensure Roni's safety in a strange land where she would have to adjust to a life without the tools she was accustomed to.

Roni sat nervously, awaiting her parents' advice.

Kimiko looked at Mihara and gave a quick nod to proceed. He hesitated at first but soon found himself without any other choice.

"I don't doubt you already know your fate," he clarified somberly. Roni gave him a slight nod. Her father then continued, "You, of course, know that you won't ever be able to return home again. You'll no longer be one of us once the transformation is complete." Sadness and loss were evident in his voice.

Roni again nodded her head and stared blankly into nowhere.

"The special powers bestowed upon us by the Creator will be taken away. You have forfeited that gift," he clarified. "The only thing you will leave with is the skills you have learned here, which you can use for your protection against a hostile world filled with cruelty and evil. You understand?"

Roni tilted her head solemnly.

Her mother couldn't bear the thought of her flesh and blood subjected to the cruel world above.

"Tell her, Mihara," she interrupted, clutching her fingers tightly.

Mihara raised his hand in acknowledgment and proceeded to explain, "There is one other thing. This is something that you, as well as most of our people here, are not aware of."

Roni jerked slightly at the mere mention of a secret. *What can it be?* She leaned forward in her father's direction, giving him her utmost attention.

"Well..." Mihara tried to go on but found himself unable to divulge what he wanted to say. It was the first time, since he became an emperor, that he was going to banish an Imen, and worse, it was his own child.

Meanwhile, Kimiko became impatient and once again cut in.

"What your father is trying to say is that there *is* somewhere you can go where you can be safe," she confided.

"There is?" Roni asked with astonishment.

"Yes, there is," affirmed her father.

"Where? Where's this place?" asked Roni incredulously.

"Patience, Roni. Patience. It's not that easy to get to. It's a journey filled with great danger, and you must be prepared for every threat," he continued.

"But where is it?" she asked impatiently.

"It's far...on the other side of the forest, over the great mountain range in the south," he stated.

Roni began to visualize the area in her head and wondered if she had ever been close to where this place was.

"How do you know about this place, Father, and who lives there?" she asked sincerely.

"I'm the Emperor. I'm privy to many things," he replied with authority.

"But how do I get there and most importantly, who lives there?" she prodded impatiently.

Roni began to feel forlorn. The thought of leaving Imen-Hera forever now had started to become real to her.

Her shoulders drooped with a sigh of resignation, and she kept her eyes cast to the ground. All this sounded unsurmountable, and her stomach was in knots as she heard her father's words. It was like nothing she had ever felt before. Everything was too foreign.

Looking at Roni's demeanor, Mihara knew he had to be the one to infuse courage in his daughter. She could not give up at any point. He locked up all his feelings tightly and in a serious tone, devoid of all emotions, he stood tall like the Emperor of Imen-Hera ought to be and spoke carefully, "My dear, you must prepare to leave in haste. Much time has passed since the beginning of your transformation, and you won't be able to stay here. You must find a safe haven in the White Forest of Bellwin."

"White Forest of Bellwin?" interrupted Roni.

"Yes, the White Forest of Bellwin," repeated her father.

"But I've never heard of such a place."

"That's right. You have not, and nor have the rest of Imen-Hera besides your mother, myself, and Miwa," he continued.

"Miwa? Why is that?" Roni asked in complete confusion.

"Now is not the moment for questions. You don't have much time. You need to pay close attention to what I am about to tell you. You cannot share this information with anyone. Not even Suki or Kenji, you understand?" he commanded in a stern voice.

"Yes. I understand," she replied as a frown marred her forehead. It was evident she was perplexed and had a hundred questions.

"It's important you realize why this is not something to share with others in Imen-Hera. The White Forest of Bellwin is a place where you'll find people who were once Imen and have lost their privilege to remain here for doing the exact same thing as you. They are just like you."

"There are others like me? Imen? Banished just like me?" she asked in complete astonishment.

"Yes, and they cannot adjust or live easily amongst the people above. They have a place of their own. Safe and away from the rest, and that's in Bellwin," he stated.

Roni was hopeful, but the fear of uncertainty continued to grip her.

"How will I know how to get there?" she asked.

"You will take a southern path following the white flower trail that will lead you to the Talbot Mountain Range. There, you will have to negotiate up its cliff."

Roni listened carefully. She had never climbed a mountain. This was going to present her with her first challenge, or so she thought.

"You will find many tiny niches concealed in the boulders. Use them to climb the sheer rock face. When you reach the top, you will find a border of dense thickets. Beyond that is the Barren."

This was too much for Roni as she struggled to focus and remember.

"You will have to make your way across the Barren, moving southeast. When you reach the far side, you'll see the White Forest. Your path will be fraught with peril, and you must take caution. Once there, you will be met by your new guardians, who will take you into their care," he explained.

"White flower trail? I've never seen such a trail, Father," she replied as she searched her memories to recall what she knew about the forest.

"It is there. You would not have noticed it unless it was mentioned prior," he replied.

"Now I have just mapped out how you are to reach your destination, and although it sounds very simple, it is a treacherous journey filled with many dangers," he warned with sorrow and regret.

"Dangers?" she asked naively.

"Yes, dangers. Wild animals, creatures, and others. There are too many things out there that you need to be aware of. It is not going to be the same as before. You will have no way of plucking an arrow from thin air anymore nor the ability to slow time to make an exit.

"You will be subject to the same things as those who dwell above. We will provide you with all the necessary tools you will need, but the rest is up to you," he explained methodically.

She pondered everything he had said and tried to remember it all. She wondered what tools he was talking about.

Although she was afraid, she was brave enough to deal with what lay before her. Roni had more questions she wanted to ask.

"I hope I can remember everything you've told me," she stated sadly.

"So do I."

"How will they know I'm one of them?" she questioned.

"The guardians will know. But right now, you must not concern yourself with such petty things. We must get on with your departure. We don't have much time," he replied.

"You need a few but necessary items that will help get you there." He then called out to his wife, "Kimiko, help me put them together."

They both got busy opening cabinets, pulling out odd things, gathering garments, and laying them all on the table.

Meanwhile, Roni sat on a nearby chair, feeling helpless, her face taut and muscles rigid. She was deeply worried about her future, which paralyzed her from doing anything. She blankly watched them pile many items on the small table in front of her.

Her parents conversed with one another, but Roni was not in tune with their conversation. Mihara added strange but somewhat familiar objects to the pile that perplexed Roni.

One of these items looked like the zoon but lacked the typical embellishments of shells, metal discs, and colorful tassels. Instead, it was made of brown leather and at both ends had small, fist-sized heavy balls encased in leather.

There was nothing fancy about this zoon, and it was clear it served a different purpose than what was used for dance and entertainment.

There was a scabbard that held two *dandum* sticks, one on each side, but these sticks had long blades at their ends. Roni wondered what these items were for but soon realized they were the tools her father had mentioned.

She began to feel ill at the thought of using them for anything other than dance.

"What's the purpose of this zoon and the blades that look like *dandum* sticks?" She lifted the zoon from the pile apprehensively.

Her parents paused in their rummage to look at the items their daughter was pointing out with great shame. These objects were central to their culture and similar to those used in almost all their dance routines. As dance props, they presented no harm to anyone.

Yet these objects were now being brandished as weapons. Harming or killing another living being went against the premier tenets of the Imen as they were bestowed with the task of healing.

Wielding a weapon that could potentially harm or kill another was forbidden but with a few exceptions. And those exceptions did not apply in Imen-Hera.

Roni relaxed her hold on the zoon and let it fall back to the pile. She was distraught. A fresh wave of fear filled her being.

What have I done?

Emperor Mihara explained their history to Roni, who sat back on her chair, listening to him in complete disbelief — yet it all made perfect sense.

"These dance instruments were once our weapons, but now we've turned them into objects of art. We transformed our fight routines into dance movements to preserve something from our past. Over the years, it has helped those like you, exiled from Imen-Hera, survive the hostilities that lie above. At least I hope they have," he explained.

Roni was left completely shaken. Never in a thousand years would she have guessed the truths her father was revealing to her. She knew nothing other than the simple, jaunty life she had led in Imen-Hera. Everything was too much for her to take in all at once. No words escaped her mouth in reply to her father.

She continued to sift through everything that had just been disclosed to her, and in the midst of it all, she remembered Eyvind. She wondered if she was going to see him once she left Imen-Hera.

Suddenly, her bleak situation didn't seem too hopeless. At least she had something to look forward to, but there was no promise of that either.

After the explanation, the Emperor and Empress instructed Ginji to summon Miwa to the royal quarters.

Meanwhile, Roni realized that she had not told Kenji or Suki about her departure.

"I can't leave without saying goodbye to Suki and Kenji. They don't know anything. Let me talk to them. Please. Just once," she pleaded.

Mihara looked at Kimiko for advice, but she remained silent. They were faced with a difficult decision because they could not allow any more delays. Furthermore, it was forbidden to impart the knowledge of her banishment to anyone until she was gone.

Roni was losing her translucent glow fast, and soon she would not be able to survive the underground conditions of Imen-Hera. She had to leave in haste, and the departure ceremony had to be performed expeditiously.

Waiting for her friends would only delay her leaving. Looking at their stony expressions, Roni felt lost and forlorn, almost frightened of what was happening to her.

"I am sorry, Roni, but you don't have much time. I wish there was a way to keep this from happening, but there isn't." Kimiko shook her head in regret.

"There isn't much time. Soon the trees won't allow you passage, and you will die a tortured death here. If you leave now, at least you'll get a chance to find a new life above. We have to hurry. Summoning Suki and Kenji will only cause further delay. I hope you understand," she explained painfully. The melancholic look on Roni's face spoke volumes.

"How can I leave without saying goodbye? I'll never see them again," she pleaded one more time.

Silence hung like a thick fog, and both of her parents were speechless. It was unbearable for them to see Roni in this mortal situation. Before they could answer, there was a gentle knock on the door. It was Miwa and Ginji. Miwa entered the chamber and stood before them.

Mihara made an exception and quietly told Ginji to summon Kenji and Suki immediately.

Roni looked at Miwa shamefully.

"Good, you are here. Let's get on with the ceremony. She doesn't have much time," Mihara stated.

Miwa gave Roni a nod to acknowledge her presence who bent her head down in embarrassment.

"Where are the artifacts?" Miwa asked somberly. She had been waiting for this moment. She was surprised that it had taken Roni this long to inform her parents. She wondered if it was already too late for her.

Kimiko pointed to the pile on the table, and Miwa came forward to examine the heap.

"Where's the armor?" she asked.

Mihara opened the back of the gigantic armoire that stood prominently against the wall in front of them and walked into it. He disappeared for a while, and Roni looked on in complete astonishment.

All this time, she had no idea there was a hidden chamber behind the armoire. Moments later, he emerged holding something wrapped in cloth.

He set it on the table, and Miwa opened the bundle and produced the garments.

Kimiko moved closer to Miwa and handed her four small white spheres.

The priestess put them on the table and instructed Roni to step forward, who came to stand before her, not knowing what to expect.

Miwa handed the garments to Roni and asked her to change into them.

She picked up the bundle and gravely walked into the adjacent room to put them on. They resembled her colorful and ornate dance attire in their form; however, these were neither colorful nor ornate. They were very muted in color and a lot heavier.

By the time she finished wearing all that was given to her, she was outfitted like a warrior ready for battle, fully clad in lamellar armor that allowed fluid motion with its rectangular scale-like pieces made from the bark of the Boad trees.

The armor covered her torso, arms, and a skirt that extended just above her knees. She had shin guards made of hardened leather that fastened over her boots. Even her gloves were covered with smaller scales to protect her hands.

When she was done dressing, she stood staring at herself in the mirror in complete horror. She was afraid and doubted if she could ever harm another being. As nagging doubts rushed through her head, there was a knock on the door.

"Roni, you don't have much time, my dear," announced her mother through the wooden frame.

Roni emerged from the room clad in the warrior garb. She looked strange and uncomfortable. There was a momentary look of shock and horror on everyone's face, but they quickly concealed it and consciously tried to control their composure.

Roni stood before them, not knowing what to expect next.

Miwa took the tiny white spheres and placed them around Roni in a square. Then she handed her the zoon, the *dandum* blades, and the helmet. Roni held on to them reluctantly.

"You better get comfortable holding them. They're your only protection against the wicked ugly world out there. These implements are the only things that will help you stay alive. Especially until you reach the White forest of Bellwin," stated Miwa.

Roni took a good look at the weapons and tried to hold them as comfortably and as naturally as she could. Tears streamed down her face; however, the others did not allow themselves to be affected by them.

Miwa held out her hand to Kimiko, who approached her quickly and placed a tiny vial in her hand.

The priestess got down to her knees and carefully placed a tiny drop of liquid from the vial on each sphere. They immediately glowed brightly and bathed Roni with an intense bluish light.

Roni was puzzled by the strange ritual and wondered about its significance.

Miwa sensed her confusion and offered an explanation. "The light will help protect you from illness and disease, among other things."

Roni had never given much thought to such inane events, and yet they were now of vital importance to her survival. Illness and disease did not exist in Imen-Hera, and Roni could not grasp the concept of facing them.

She continued to be bathed in the light for a while, and then suddenly, it vanished and so did the spheres.

Mihara took the helmet from Roni and placed it on her head. It fit snugly against her scalp, and a nosepiece extended down to cover the bridge of her nose. It had a visor that shielded her eyes. The helmet was made of a strong material covered with toughened dark brown leather on the outside. Tiny rivets held the various pieces together and also created an embellishing pattern.

At the top of the helmet, a comb of grey and white feathers swept straight back. There were three overlapping panels of neck guards, one on the back and two on either side.

He stepped back to look at her. She was a stark reminder of the days they wanted to put behind.

Kimiko couldn't bear the thought that her daughter was clad in regalia that represented their ugly and shameful past.

The awkwardness that gripped everyone was interrupted by a gentle knock on the door, followed by the entry of Kenji and Suki. They halted in their steps when they took in Roni's attire. They were both in a state of complete shock as they stood staring at their friend. Silence permeated the room. Nobody knew what to say.

They respectfully bowed and greeted the Emperor, Empress, and High Priestess before approaching Roni. Suki was completely confused. "Roni? Why're you dressed this way?" She stepped closer. "What's going on here?" There was no response. Suki turned around and looked at the others in the room for an answer.

"My dear Suki and Kenji," began Kimiko, "you were both summoned here to bid farewell to Roni."

"Farewell?" Suki cried out in shock. "Where're you going?" She turned to address Roni. Again, there was no reply.

Tears streamed down Roni's face.

Suki drew closer to her and touched the tears with her fingers and looked very puzzled. "What's this? What's happening to her? Why are you dressed like this?" she asked in terror.

Kenji remained where he stood. He had secretly known about Roni's fate but had suppressed it the entire time, refusing to accept the truth that was staring him in his face. He had been in complete denial.

It wasn't long before Mihara jumped in to inform them of Roni's banishment. He was careful to not tell them about Bellwin.

They were both stunned at the turn of events.

Suki felt silly, and guilty, for thinking Roni's recent strange behavior was related to Kenji. She suddenly recollected the encounter with the hunter—Eyvind—realizing it must have been his thoughts consuming Roni all along.

Kenji knew of this from the beginning. The hunter was the center of Roni's sin, but he couldn't blame Eyvind for the transformation in Roni, as it was she who had violated the sacred law.

The trio hugged one another tightly for a few moments. No one said a thing as Roni continued to sob quietly.

"It's time to go," Kimiko announced as she placed her hand on Roni's shoulder.

The tight embrace between the friends was broken, and a somber mood fell upon them.

"You may bid her farewell now," said Miwa to Kenji and Suki as they stepped back and moved to one side with Kenji's arm supporting a trembling Suki.

"May we go with her to the top just to keep her company for the final time?" asked Kenji.

Miwa sternly stated, "No."

They were both devastated and in a state of complete numbness.

Suki felt torn and lost. She was losing her best friend forever. She would have fallen to the ground, if not for Kenji's arm. He held her tightly against his chest and consoled her. He could feel both Roni's and Suki's pain. All of them had so much to say, yet none could find the right words. Their silence spoke volumes.

Miwa instructed Roni to follow her and led her out of the chamber.

Mihara and Kimiko slowly followed, leaving Suki and Kenji behind.

Roni looked back at her best friends for one final time as she was led away. She was seized with terror, but she held herself together and accepted her fate.

She was led through strange secret passageways that she never knew existed until they reached a small, brightly lit chamber.

Once inside, they awaited Miwa's lead. Miwa's stoic composure remained unchanged. She pulled a lever that was neatly concealed in the rough-hewn walls, releasing a staircase. She stepped back and allowed the Emperor and Empress to bid their child farewell.

Kimiko hugged her tightly and wiped her tear-soaked face. Her daughter looked so strange dressed in the ancient warrior regalia.

"My dear, dear child…" She embraced her tightly against her bosom and rocked her back and forth.

"You were never meant for us, and this is the price we chose to pay when I forced Miwa's hand and asked for a child. You were promised elsewhere, and that's where your destiny lies. Forgive us for bringing you this pain. I shouldn't have tried to bend the hand of fate for my selfish desires. If only I had resisted. If only there was a way to help you…" she lamented.

"You have to accept responsibility for your decisions. Once made, one should accept the good and bad that come with it. Everything is a lesson learned. Regrets are for the fickle," spoke Miwa with wisdom.

"You're right, Miwa, but had I understood the gravity of this loss, I would have chosen otherwise," she replied.

"Your decision brought you many years of pleasure, did it not?" asked Miwa.

Kimiko nodded her head. "It most certainly did. And it is also bringing the greatest of pain with it. Not only for me but also for my daughter."

She approached Roni and looked into her eyes and spoke softly, "I would do it again but only if I could save you from this. The happiness you have brought us for the past seventy years cannot be replaced by anything. I never imagined this pleasure would come to an abrupt end in such a short time. But I'm grateful for the years we've had with you."

Kimiko was instantly reminded of the lifespan of those living above. It was different from that of the Imen. She abruptly turned to Miwa. "How long will she live above? Also, she's much older than those there. She won't die, will she?"

"No, she will not. She is protected. She will be of the same age. However, she will also die around the same age as them. She is now one of them and no longer of us," she explained.

The Imen lived for at least four hundred years on average and some close to five.

Eventually, they transformed into light spheres to join the Creator. Over time, as they joined Him, their numbers would slowly begin to dwindle.

A day would arrive when there would be none left, and those like Roni, who were cast out from Imen-Hera, would carry forward their crafts and skills.

Mihara stepped closer to bid his child farewell. He had remained silent the entire time, keeping his loss to himself. He held Roni tightly and kissed her on the forehead.

"My dear child, you've been the light of my life, and you'll always shine brightly. Go now and take with you the skills and art of our proud people. Someday, when the last of the Imen departs to join the Creator, we'll be remembered through you and the others."

Roni had never imagined having such a conversation with her father.

He continued with his words of wisdom. "Put your skills to good use and transform ill deeds into virtuous ones. Help them change their ways, but don't become one of them. You're of Imen blood and never forget this. Preserve our ways. Can you promise me that?" he asked.

"Yes. I promise," Roni replied. She found her father's words comforting.

"Then I bid you safe passage to Bellwin." He kissed her again on the forehead as his final act of goodbye.

Roni felt Miwa's attention on her. It was time. She wiped her face and looked at the stairs, but before she made her way up, her gaze fell on the ring on her finger.

The magnificent blue stone glistened brightly. She started to remove it, not knowing if she should leave it behind, but Mihara stopped her.

Just as she turned to ascend, Kimiko called out to her one last time. "Take this gift." She removed a tiny glass vial that hung around her neck, by a delicate string, and put it around Roni's neck.

"If you're ever in need, this will help see you to safety. Use it wisely, and may the Creator forever shroud you from danger." She kissed her daughter for the last time, and with that, Roni climbed up the narrow stairs until she disappeared, her back firm and her demeanor stoic.

Mihara held Kimiko closely as they stood in the chamber with their gaze transfixed on the vacant stairs.

Several moments passed, and then Miwa broke the silence by closing the stairwell shut. With a pull of the lever, the steps vanished.

She turned and disappeared down the passageway, leaving Mihara and Kimiko clutching each other silently.

DEEP IN THE WOODS, a grumble echoed in the air along with heavy footsteps and rustling of leaves.

Bomo shoved the branches and shrubs out of his way as he propelled through the forest in anger, having failed to obtain the Lightning Rose. It was his one and only chance, and he had bungled it up by falling asleep.

He stamped the ground and kicked at the roots, blaming everything that came his way. He cursed and spat, throwing his fists up in the air as he walked along. He wasn't certain where he was going, but he kept moving aimlessly.

At times, he followed the trail of the riders, but he tried to not stay on it in case he accidentally ran into them. That would lead to certain death.

Time passed, and the sun arced across the great sky and hovered almost directly above.

Bomo had been on the move for a few hours, so he decided to rest for a while. He had no provisions with him, nor had he thought of food all day.

His mind was fixed on the Lightning Rose that had gotten away.

The ogre kicked some leaves into a pile and plopped himself down. His golden-yellow eyes searched the ground for any edible morsel he could find but came up empty. This added fuel to the fire and made him angrier.

He swore until he was out of breath and beat the ground with his fists in a fit of rage. And as he continued to violently pound the ground, he noticed something flickering at a distance.

He ceased his madness momentarily and remained motionless to see what it could be.

Is it somefing to eat? He wondered in his mind, hoping for a meal.

He got down on his hands and knees and crawled, keeping his bulky body low to the forest bed, and made his way toward it. The ogre dug his calloused elbows into the ground and awkwardly pulled himself forward. As he got closer, he still wasn't able to make out what it was.

It 'as to be a little animal, an' if I sneak up to it, I might be able to catch it with me bare 'ands, an' it'll make a fine lunch. He began to salivate at the idea of some food.

Bomo lacked the prowess to sneak up on anything. The only way he could catch something was either by trapping it or knocking it to death by hurling a rock at it.

The idiot ogre imagined himself to be a great hunter and continued to drag his heavy frame along the ground in the direction of his intended prey, lifting his head intermittently to ascertain he was moving in the right direction. To his amazement, his target remained stationary.

Bomo grew confident of his skills, especially since he had evaded detection so far. He was now only a few feet away from it, and still, no movement could be detected.

Bomo wondered if the animal was dead since it remained motionless. He wasn't sure what to expect or do.

Suddenly, the one lone cell in his cranium flickered and asked him a question. *Wot if it's stalkin' me?*

In that instant, he decided to pounce on it before it jumped on him.

The bumbling specimen thrust himself up in the air, leaped forward, and finally came crashing down upon it with a big thud.

To his surprise, it was not an animal or an insect. Neither was it any other creature at all.

What he had stumbled upon was the Lightning Rose. Luckily, not all of his bulk had fallen on it. He had managed to just half-crush the delicate flower.

"There it is!" he exclaimed.

He pushed himself up to his knees and stared at it with his demonic yellow eyes. His mouth agape, he bore caution to not breathe upon it.

Bomo stared at it in complete disbelief.

"Wot fate!" he cried out. "That's the same one thay 'ad. I suffered for this all night. Thay must've bungled it. Now it's mine."

He carried on with his madness and chattered nonstop for a while before he realized the guards could return in case it was they who had accidentally dropped it.

He immediately got up, snatched the rose off the ground, tucked it in his tattered shirt, and hurried back home.

The fiend mumbled his wicked plans all the way as he trampled through the forest. This time in glee.

"She'll be mine soon, an' I'll 'ave more gold…as much as I could want. Ha, ha, ha, ha, ha, ha!"

THE NIGHT WAS LONG and awkward for Eyvind. He was facing a difficult dilemma that presented no solution.

Several times during the evening, his father had extolled the union. Yet, each time Eyvind looked at Adina, he felt increasingly uncomfortable. There was no way he could go on with the marriage as planned, at least not under these circumstances.

Also, Eyvind's attention was distracted by his soldiers' search for Laris.

In the midst of it all, there was something else that gnawed at his insides, which he was unable to pinpoint. He snuck away from the festivities many times to wander around, trying to resolve what was bothering him.

Being a soldier, it was second nature to him to be suspicious of everyone and never let his guard down. To distract his mind from the ongoing problems, he found himself keeping his eyes on every Carthinian in attendance.

The night slowly wore down, and everyone retired to their designated chambers except for Eyvind, who decided to stay up for a while and walk the perimeter of the castle and its grounds. In one of his many forays, he saw something that caused him to stop in his tracks and hide behind a pillar in a hallway. He thought he saw shadows skulking around, but when he peeked once more, he couldn't find anything.

Is my mind playing tricks on me?

He shook the thought away and searched other corridors for any moving shadows. He went to the soldier guarding a hallway and spoke from behind him, "Guard, did you see anyone moving about?"

The man was startled and stumbled forward, then turned around. Seeing his half-mast eyes, it was obvious to Eyvind that he had been drifting off to sleep. Alarm rose within him, and shaking his head, he repeated the question.

"N-no, Sire. N-no one," the half-sleepy soldier managed to stutter.

Screaming at the man in the middle of the night would only lead to further embarrassment, and the young prince was sure his father would be most displeased about it. He decided to hold his tongue and question a few more soldiers on duty. Each denied having seen anyone, which made Eyvind extremely angry at how lax everyone had become. He called for the main guard and ordered a more vigilant watch and multiple rounds of patrolling.

At this point, he understood what he had to do next—a decision that was his duty.

The following morning, Eyvind decided to meet his father before the resumption of festivities with the guests and any further discussions. He hadn't slept much the previous night as his thoughts kept racing from one problem to the other. He needed to inform the King about Korin and Adina. He also wanted to bring to his attention his suspicions about the Carthinians.

So, he rushed to catch his father before it was too late. He opened the door to the king's chamber and stopped abruptly on seeing the sight before him. His parents were engaged in an argument regarding Adina and him, which they immediately ceased upon his entrance.

That made it easy for him to address the awkward topic.

"Eyvind? Up so early?" inquired his mother nervously.

"Yes…I've been up for a while. I didn't mean to overhear your conversation, but it leads into what I need to talk to you both about," he replied.

"Don't you dare try to back out! I know where you're going with this," barked Audun. "There'll be no further discussion on this topic, you hear me? Both you and your mother have no understanding of diplomatic arrangements."

"Father…" Eyvind tried to explain when he was abruptly interrupted.

"I said, there'll be no further discussion on this topic. You understand?" Audun growled in sheer annoyance at his son's protests.

"But…but there's something I must bring to your attention regarding this arrangement," Eyvind tried again.

"I can guess what that could be. Let me see. No romance? She's not pretty enough for you? I dread to find out what sort of flaws you've come up with," Audun stated in disgust.

Eyvind sighed in frustration and wondered if this was indeed the right time to discuss Adina. Instead, he decided to turn tracks and inform his father of what he had witnessed last night. "I suppose I should bring the bigger and more urgent issue to your attention then."

"What issue would that be?" Audun asked sarcastically.

"I spent last night surveilling the grounds and found several Carthinians sneaking around in the dark. I think we're being spied upon. They appeared to be studying our layout and guard positions. They're up to something. I don't trust them."

"That's the most pathetic excuse, even for you, to try to sabotage this pact. I should've made this arrangement with your brother instead. Perhaps then I wouldn't have half of these problems. Do you understand the position you're putting me in?" he yelled at his son.

"I'm well aware of it and understand more than I'm given credit for," replied Eyvind curtly.

"No. You don't understand. Don't tell me you do because we wouldn't be engaged in this discussion if you did!" he screamed, pointing his finger in Eyvind's face.

Queen Beyla was in a state of shock. She had never seen the king so enraged. She knew it was best to remain silent because her viewpoint was considered inconsequential by her husband. This was clearly a father-son issue, and she had to stay out of it.

"Maybe you should have arranged this union between Korin and Adina. After all, he is her lover." Eyvind didn't want to back down anymore.

"How dare you insult your brother and Adina! Have you gone mad?" the king snapped.

"Eyvind! We won't tolerate such sordid remarks, especially when they involve your brother," added Queen Beyla angrily.

Eyvind was now up against both his parents, seeing that his intended conversation had derailed. He thought hard about how to return it to civil terms and tried again in a polite voice. "I apologize for my outburst, but there's something urgent I need to tell you. It is the truth. Both Korin and Adina are bound to each other, and neither knows the true identity of the other."

"Impossible! Seamy lies! Is this what we are to expect from you, Eyvind?" snarled the King.

"What makes you so sure?" asked Queen Beyla, looking at her son.

"Mother, she's wearing a charm on her bracelet that could have only come from Korin. It's one of a kind. He told me so when I saw it on him. Only he has that charm, and now it is with her," Eyvind put forth his point.

"Fool! You came to this conclusion based on a charm? You have gone mad. Insane!" Audun clutched his head with both hands and walked around the room in disbelief, tugging at his hair in frustration.

"No, Father, I didn't base it on a charm," Eyvind shot back in defense. "Didn't you notice her demeanor at dinner after she walked through the portrait hall? It was as though she'd seen a ghost. She was so mortified she couldn't even eat and chose to go outside, fearing an encounter with him. And it wasn't until she was told Korin wasn't here that she decided to come back in and rejoin the festivities."

At first, King Audun tried to not listen to him, but as Eyvind continued to explain, he began to remember the events his son mentioned. Keeping his back to him, he thought hard and long about Adina's behavior the night before. The more he recalled everything, the more he realized the plausibility of Eyvind's statement. He turned and faced him, listening to his words, but remained silent while he digested the shocking news.

"Believe me, I'll never let you down, but you have to understand this. I simply cannot marry a woman who's in love with my brother. It's unfortunate, but it is so. I just cannot. I hope you can appreciate my dilemma."

On hearing this, King Audun's face became crimson in fury. He could see everything come crashing down right before his eyes. Tension built up in his body, making his muscles rigid. His hands clenched into fists as he tried to put a lid on his anger. It was all he could do to not hit his son for spoiling his plans. He was well aware there were many issues Eyvind did not see eye to eye with him. This marriage was now obviously going to be one of them.

Eyvind could only guess what his father's response was going to be. And he was not wrong. The King ranted and screamed without giving him time to explain.

"Is it possible that I raised two unfit sons? Maybe this is a bad dream from which I'll soon wake up."

"I wish it were a nightmare from which we could both wake up, but..." Eyvind was interrupted.

"But what? What? If you hadn't wasted your time hunting and gallivanting, and had instead learned how to rule a nation, we'd never be in this predicament. You hear me?"

"Audun, please!" Queen Beyla interjected.

"I need you to stay out of this, Beyla. I have enough to deal with right now," he countered.

Enraged, Beyla stormed out of the chamber.

"So, it's my fault. You may think I'm out gallivanting, Father, but have you ever wondered how our borders are kept secure? Did you ever give a thought to why our neighbors are unable to spy on us? No, you don't know, do you?"

"Don't be foolish. We haven't spared any expense in getting the best-trained guards, and that's how we're able to secure our borders," Audun barked back.

"Is that what you think? You really think it stops there, Father? All the well-trained guards can be bought. How do you think we get information about our neighbors? They too have well-trained guards."

"So what? Even if our borders are penetrated, we can defend ourselves. We stand unmatched," flaunted King Audun.

"Is that what you think?" asked Eyvind in disbelief. "You just invited the enemy into your house, and already they've studied our defenses and weaknesses by sneaking around in the middle of the night. How do you know they won't launch an attack the moment they get back?" he questioned.

"Don't be ridiculous," Audun smirked in a superior tone. "Do you think I've idly sat by and not thought about that? You think I trust these people just because we have an agreement? Korin has been spying on our guests secretly. We're a few steps ahead of their game."

Eyvind was shocked, but in reality, nothing should have surprised him about his father and brother. They had been doing this their whole life. He felt complete disgust with his father's tactics and wondered what they were up to and if he should be worried. But he didn't have to try very hard to figure out that his father might be planning a future invasion of his neighbor.

"Isn't the purpose of this so-called union—to have peace between our nations and end the bloodshed?"

Audun laughed at his son's naivety. "Why am I not surprised? Have you no drive for power or control? Do you know how strong our nation will be if we form this union?" There was glee written all over his face.

"No. No, I don't. At least not the way you're going about it. And when were you planning on informing me about this underhanded plan?" he asked angrily.

"If you were more involved in the affairs of the ruling, you'd know a lot more. And, for your information, this is the only way of assuming control and acquiring more power. Meanwhile, I can't seem to accomplish even the first phase." Audun gave his son a pointed look.

"Can't accomplish? Father, she's in love with Korin. How can you expect me to marry her? I'll renounce my claim to the throne if I have to. I won't be part of your phony peace peddling. It's a sham!"

"How dare you!"

"What else do you call it?"

"You haven't the slightest idea of what this nation is embarking on. This is precisely why you aren't privy to this information. You are unworthy!" the King shouted back.

"Unworthy? I've carried out my duties with a pure heart. Now I find out I've sold lies to these people. Our people! I've won their confidence and trust in me. It's a matter of integrity, Father. And why should you care anyway? It wasn't you who peddled the lies to them," he blasted his father angrily.

"Don't be so melodramatic, Eyvind. You don't need to preach lessons of integrity to me. You and your mother…both clutching archaic virtues of a long-gone era. There's no room for them in this day and age."

"Call them what you want. Those are the standards I live by."

"And it'll be the fall of you. It's all part of being a powerful ruler. It's cut or get cut, and romantic notions will only get you cut."

"I refuse to forsake them. I'd rather renounce my claim to the throne. Let Korin be the heir. After all, he's in love with Adina, and he sees eye to eye with you on your plans of invasion and expansion and whatever else you have schemed," Eyvind stated in dismay.

"You've failed me, Eyvind. I had underlying doubts about you from the very start, but I tried to convince myself otherwise. I'm glad it's at this juncture you've revealed your unworthiness. It's precisely why you were never included in these discussions because I was afraid you'd object and fail to carry out your duties," Audun replied coldly.

"It's good to know your faith and trust in me were so expansive. Well, I'm not a puppet." Eyvind shook his head in utter disbelief.

"It's nothing to bemoan about. You made the choice, not I. If you choose to renounce your claim to the throne, then so be it," the King replied without emotion.

"You used me, Father. You knew all this, and yet you still used me." Eyvind couldn't believe the coldness in his father's voice and the words he was spouting.

"The deck of life is stacked with hard lessons, and if you aren't up for the challenge, then you can only expect disappointment and defeat. It's a measure by which the devoted are weeded out from the dispensable. You've made a wise decision to surrender your claim. Then again, I wouldn't have expected you to put up a fuss," the King derided him.

"What if I had refused?" Eyvind dared to ask.

"You wouldn't have. Trust me." There was complete confidence in the King's words.

Eyvind saw a side of his father he had never seen before, though he had suspected it was present. "Then I suppose my job here is done since I am dispensable," he replied in a sarcastic tone. He pretended to be unaffected, but he felt a lump in his throat that he couldn't swallow and a hollowed out pain in his abdomen. The binding tie between his father and him had severed. Everything in him hurt as he felt the dual thrusts of his father's icy attitude and outright rejection.

He was unsure of where to go or what to do. He was an outcast now. He remained standing in front of his father for a moment, looking at him and processing what had transpired.

The uncomfortable silence was interrupted by a thunderous knock on the door. A soldier, out of breath, burst in. "They…they are here. The Imperial Knights."

The king had no idea why the Knights deserved such attention. "What Knights? From where?"

"They're returning from the forest, and it seems they have found Lord Laris, Your Highness," the soldier replied timidly.

"Found Lord Laris? What's this all about?" he questioned.

Eyvind didn't waste time dashing out to greet his men. A gamut of emotions flowed through his mind. He hoped his friend had been found alive, but a nagging feeling within him indicated a different result.

The soldier tried to rush out with Eyvind, but an order stopped him dead in his tracks.

"Halt!" King Audun yelled out to the soldier, who turned to face the King.

Audun wondered what his elder son had been up to and, whatever it was, if it was going to affect his plans.

"Your Highness?" the soldier replied.

"What's this all about?"

"Your Majesty, the Imperial Knights left yesterday to search for Lord Laris, and they are now returning with him."

"To search for Lord Laris?" the King asked in utter confusion. "Stop speaking in riddles and start from the beginning. What happened to him?"

"Your Majesty, he went missing a few days ago, and Prince Eyvind went searching for him yesterday only to find out that he'd taken off into the woods. So, a search party went to look for him," he answered innocently.

"Went missing? Why would he go missing?" Audun was baffled by the soldier's utterances. He wondered what evil plans Laris had been up to and became worried.

"I don't know why, Your Majesty," he replied with sincerity.

Audun pushed the soldier out of his way and rushed out to find Eyvind. He hurried down the hallways to find out what this was all about.

Meanwhile, Eyvind saddled his horse Jet and tore through Jasper to meet the approaching party. He could see them at a distance. He whipped his horse to move faster, but time stood still with each gallop forward. It seemed to take an eternity.

King Audun called out for Aurelius, who appeared immediately, and informed him of what had just transpired.

The minister was shocked to hear the news, but not surprised. He had harbored disdain toward Eyvind from the start and considered him an impediment to their plans. In the past, he had tried to let the king know without being too intrusive but wasn't able to convince him implicitly.

Aurelius now seized the opportunity to blast Eyvind's sincerity.

Audun instructed him to spy on his son as well as the Imperial Knights and find out what they had been up to. Nothing could get in the way of their plans.

The minister departed from the chamber and summoned his spies to follow Eyvind and gather information.

EYVIND RACED TOWARD THE distant blurred figures, urging his horse Jet faster, until they began to take shape as he drew closer. His breath hitched in anticipation. He could hardly wait to see his friend. But as he approached them, it became apparent that one of the horses carried a slumped body. His mind tried to evade the truth, but he had to see with his own eyes to believe it.

Finally, he reached the somber party and came to an abrupt stop, jumping off Jet at lightning speed. The Imperial Knights came to a halt in front of their Prince, their melancholic expressions revealing everything. No one said a word. What could they say in the light of this turn of events?

Eyvind approached Laris's horse apprehensively, his fingers trembling as he gently lifted the cloak from the bloodied and flaccid body.

Laris' dusky face, icy cold to the touch, revealed a violent struggle. Tears welled in

Eyvind's eyes as a thousand emotions and questions raced through his mind.

He clenched his fists and bent his head, searching deep in his core for the control that every Imperial Knight was famous for. His teeth sank into his lips as he mourned the loss of his friend. Raidon and Axel stood on either side of him in silent support. Eyvind was horrified that Laris had indeed died a violent death.

Slowly and steadily, the fire of his rage built up deep within him as questions ran through his mind, demanding answers. He turned to Raidon for answers when the sounds of the fast gallop reached his ears. Moments later, the soldiers sent by King Audun pulled the reins of their horses, causing them to come to a abrupt stop before Eyvind and the Imperial Knights.

Shane, the leader, dismounted and approached seeing that Laris had fallen. He looked askance at the Knights, casting his glance all around, but not a word of an explanation was spoken.

"How did this happen?" he enquired, now addressing Raidon and Axel.

Silence persisted, and neither offered a reply.

Eyvind sensed Shane had been sent by the King to spy on him. He walked back to his horse, mounted and began to cantor toward the castle. The Knights too did the same and followed their Prince. Eyvind wanted to get Laris back to Jasper and then set off to search for the party responsible. He pushed his horse to a fast gallop as anger continued to build within him, threatening to singe him completely.

Shane and his party meekly followed behind. On reaching Jasper, all of them began to wind their way up to the castle. The townsmen came out of their homes and stood by the side of the road to stare at the solemn procession, seeing the slumped body but unaware of the identity of the departed.

Eyvind perceived a strange vibe emanating from the soldiers sent by the King to escort them back. He surreptitiously peeked back at them several times to see what they were up to. He did not like the unfurling of this event that he was subjected to but decided to hold his tongue for now.

Coming closer to the castle, the entire procession was halted by Aurelius, who stood in their path along with a few of his soldiers.

Eyvind detested his father's advisor with a fervor. Aurelius was despicable and conniving, a person completely devoid of morals and values. He was always in his father's ear, making suggestions and recommending policies. They were usually strategies that best served the King and himself. Aurelius was possessed by the demon of greed. Exactly the kind of man his father liked to favor. And the kind of man that the young Prince detested to cross paths with. Unless the man stood directly in his way.

Eyvind was annoyed at being stopped by him and made no qualms about showing it. With a blank expression, looking back at Aurelius' soldiers in the rear, he stated, "It's a slain Knight. There was no need to send your goons to spy on us for that."

The riders at the back became embarrassed for having carried out such a dirty task against Eyvind.

A dark expression flitted across Aurelius' eyes before he managed to school his expression and pretended to be oblivious about the accusation, going on to show feigned concern. "Spy, Your Highness? What would possess you to think I would need to spy on the Prince? I was merely concerned about you and alarmed at the way you rushed out. I sent the men to help escort you back safely." Shaking his head in a regretful manner, while holding a slight smirk on his lips, he added, "It's a pity you have such a dim opinion of me."

Eyvind knew the man was lying and possessed not a single iota of goodwill toward him or the rest of his Knights. In lieu of a protracted argument that would get him nowhere, he chose to take care of the business at hand. He pushed his way through Aurelius' soldiers without comment and rode back to the castle.

Some of the townspeople and guards stopped mid-work and looked at them in horror. No one dared to ask who it was. They merely lowered their heads in respect as the procession rode through.

The Imperial Knights reached a small courtyard at the back of the castle. One of the buildings there was the house of worship—a tall, ornate edifice that served the royal family. The entire structure was circular and tapered as it rose to the sky, with a glass dome crowning its top.

The lower third of this building had no windows, just sculptures carved into the walls depicting the ancient history of the Carronites. The upper two-thirds was pierced with hundreds of tiny windows that allowed light and air to filter through the structure much like a sieve.

When the sun was at its zenith, its rays flooded light through the dome and down its center, illuminating the altar. Around the periphery of the altar were rows of seats carved from rare and expensive white stone. Outlying rooms surrounded the inner sanctum of worship, and these were used by the priests, some to live and some to house artifacts.

There were north, south, east, and west entrances that led the way into and out of the structure. Ornate flying buttresses functioned as fins for the harmonics of the sound produced by the enormous pipe organ within. And thereby it could be heard far and wide.

Appropriate entrances were used depending on the ceremony. The south door was used for funerals, and the north door, for births. The east door was for unhappy events, whereas the west was for celebrations such as weddings and victories.

Eyvind dismounted outside this dignified structure and went to Laris' slumped body, reaching out to hold his dear friend in his arms for one final time. Accompanied by Raidon and Axel, he carried Laris through the south doorway and into the belly of the building until he reached the inner sanctum. He moved toward the circular altar and placed Laris' body upon a round stone table set at the center.

Raidon looked all over and leaned back to whisper to Axel. "Where's the Lightning Rose?"

Axel looked under the cloak that had covered Laris, but there was no sign of it. "I tucked it in the strap when we started from the forest. I wonder if it fell out. I'll have a look around." He walked out to search for it, but in vain could not find it anywhere. "It must have fallen somewhere along the journey," he muttered in dismay when he returned to the altar.

The high priest heard voices coming from the sacred chamber and rushed in to see what the commotion was all about. He was alarmed to find out a Knight had fallen and rushed back with a ceremonial cloth to drape over the deceased and cover the body while the rest stood by watching silently.

Within moments, King Audun strode in with Aurelius in tow to find out what had occurred. "You better have a good explanation for this, Eyvind! What happened to him?"

"He was slain. Brutally," Eyvind replied quietly.

"Slain? By whom? And why?" the King countered.

Raidon took a small step forward, bowing his head down in respect. "We think we know who did it, but we're not certain why, Your Highness."

"Who did this?" the King demanded.

"A woodcutter, but we aren't absolutely sure."

"Not sure? Expert trackers like you all, and you're not sure? And why would a simple woodcutter take a soldier's life? That doesn't make sense." The King couldn't believe his ears and was beyond furious by this time. His penetrating eyes bored into each one of the Imperial Knights, not sparing any.

"We'll be returning to the forest to track him down and find out the reason, Your Highness," assured Raidon in a calm voice.

"How…how many of you went looking for Laris? Eight? Nine? Yet you couldn't spare two or three of your men to track down this woodcutter? The very moment you discovered the body?" the King shouted. Derision emanated from each word that he screamed aloud. Audun was suspicious of this group of men and extremely furious. To lose a Knight at this point in his strategy when the Carthinians were in the palace was more than he could tolerate.

He wanted to find out every detail of what they had been up to.

Raidon answered the King. "I thought it fit to bring Laris back as a priority, Your Highness." He was aware that no matter the decision, Audun would find fault. The King was on a warpath, and heads would roll, starting with Eyvind and his soldiers.

"Fit? Priority?" Audun huffed. "By the time you get back there, the tracks would have vanished. Didn't you think about that, Raidon?"

"Your Highness, we're quite confident we can find him despite that. It won't be too difficult."

"But first, tell me, what would a woodcutter possibly want from him?" asked Aurelius, his eyes narrowed, suspicion radiating from them.

Raidon thought about explaining all the events that had occurred from the time the young Prince was injured but sensed his explanation would meet with rebuttal, no matter how logical it was. "We're not certain, Sire, but we'll depart immediately to get the answers and the woodcutter," he replied respectfully and motioned Axel to follow him.

Just as they turned to leave, Audun stopped them with a demand for more explanation about what happened to Laris.

Aurelius too gestured his guards to block the doorway to prevent the Knights from leaving.

Raidon and Axel were shocked by this swift turn of events. They had done nothing wrong. However, they couldn't dispute and go against the King's advisor. They too disliked Aurelius, but never had they imagined he would turn against them like this. They complied silently, standing still in their places, looking at Aurelius and the King in confusion.

"Your Majesty?" asked Raidon.

Aurelius moved toward them with his thin finger pointed accusingly at them. "Not so fast, gentlemen. You haven't finished explaining what Laris was doing in the forest. Now, let's start from the beginning, shall we? This time, why not tell us the whole truth?"

Audun allowed Aurelius to pose questions in his stead and extract the answers from the soldiers. The King had a deep suspicion something else was afoot, and he wanted to get to the bottom of it.

Raidon and Axel didn't know how to answer Aurelius' question without getting entangled in the web of further interrogations that would need breaking of confidences.

"So…what was Laris doing in the forest… by himself?" Aurelius repeated his question with great interest, relishing each moment of their squirming.

This style of interrogation irritated Eyvind to no end. He immediately stepped in to defend his friends. "I refuse to have my men treated with such indignity and have them questioned like common criminals. They've done nothing wrong. They need to track down this woodcutter, or whoever was responsible, without further delay."

"Surely, they can answer a couple of questions. They're master trackers, so they shouldn't have too much trouble in finding that woodcutter even if they are slightly delayed. Isn't that so?" Aurelius smirked, using the talents of these Knights against them.

"You'll let them go immediately," insisted Eyvind, standing his ground.

King Audun intervened. "And I demand answers to what you all have been up to so far and the circumstances that led to this suspicious death!"

In this chaos, the priest had stood still, obeying silence, trying to not interrupt at first, but as the conversation escalated and became a screaming match, he was forced to intercept and put his foot down. The holy sanctum was not the place for quarrels or interrogations of this nature.

"Your Majesty, I beg your pardon. I must ask that such matters be discussed elsewhere. This," he pointed to the sacred altar and the area around it, "is clearly not the appropriate place for discussing such dark matters." His voice turned to a plead by the time he was finished.

The King nodded and motioned everyone to move out. He had forgotten where they were standing. The priest bowed graciously and waited for them to exit, thanking the stars above that the sanctum had not been sullied by bloodshed.

"We'll continue below," Audun ordered as he led the way out, followed by Aurelius, who gestured his soldiers to keep watch on Eyvind and closely escort Raidon and Axel.

Eyvind was extremely annoyed at seeing his men treated like this and decided to stop this line of irrational questioning. Wanting to object to his father's insistence, he rushed to him and tried to cut the explanations short. "Father, I can tell you everything you need to know. These men need to leave and bring back those responsible for this heinous deed. The light will fade fast today." He continued to plead for his men, but the King rebuffed his efforts.

"I'm sure they do, Eyvind. However, this won't take much time at all, will it, Aurelius?" he replied without looking at Eyvind.

The cold shoulder given by his father was obvious to everyone, and the soldiers did not know where to look. Only Aurelius took great pleasure in this insult.

Eyvind was enraged. "This has something to do with our conversation from this morning, doesn't it, Father?" His frustration kept mounting as he felt his father's wickedness and cold intolerance for those who didn't see eye to eye with him.

He shook his head as he realized that anyone connected with him would now be subjected to his father's suspicion and cruelty. He knew but couldn't do a thing about it. The King was a rule onto himself.

Audun refused to dignify Eyvind's accusation with an answer and continued his march down the stairs to the dungeon below. Eyvind was frustrated and unsure of what to do. He wondered if his own fate was also in the dungeons and what would become of his men in the face of his incarceration. Or maybe it would be exile. He was prepared for it because he could no longer serve a regime whose goals and efforts were diametrically opposed to his.

Now he feared for his men. Raidon and Axel were his best friends and comrades. But he could not ask them for their support. They had sworn their loyalty and vowed to serve Carron. Now it would be up to them to choose their own paths. They may not even get the choice of exile but would have to face execution if they chose to desert their duty.

So many thoughts and so little time to decide. At last, they reached the dungeons, which were set in the deep cavernous belly of the castle that now served to store food, equipment, and artillery. On the far side were unused quarters where convicts were once interrogated before being sent off to prison or executed.

The men were led to one of the larger chambers. The heavy doors were slammed shut and bolted once all the men were in. Eyvind sensed trouble and wondered if they were ever going to leave this place alive.

The King instructed Raidon, Axel, and Eyvind to sit down in a row in front while he and Aurelius stood before them firing their questions.

"Now, let's have your story from the beginning," started Aurelius.

"What do you mean from the beginning?" asked Eyvind, his tone conveying utter annoyance, as he got up and stood face to face with Aurelius.

The King's advisor was intimidated by him and was aware of Eyvind's superior fighting skills. He tried to maintain his composure, but Audun noticed the expression of fear in Aurelius' eyes and stepped in at once.

"Sit down, Eyvind!" he yelled out. However, Eyvind remained standing, staring steadfastly at Aurelius' face, and refused to back down.

"I don't have to answer to him, Father. Since when did I start taking orders from him?" he yelled.

"Since I tell you to. Do you understand? You best sit down, Eyvind. You're no longer protected by your title. You renounced the throne, remember? You're now an ordinary citizen and will be treated as such. So, you will answer his questions," commanded Audun, which caused Aurelius to huff out loud in delight.

Eyvind wanted to pound Aurelius' face with his clenched fist, but Raidon was quick to act. He grabbed his friend's wrist and stopped it in time.

Aurelius was stunned. He winced and took an involuntary step back. He was a coward at heart who could only work in the shadow of his King.

King Audun's words pounded in Eyvind's ears. He had now heard it from his father's mouth and couldn't *unhear* it even if he wanted to—he was just an ordinary citizen. Not a Prince, not even his son, just an ordinary person of Carron. He took a deep breath in and began to process what had been said to him. He sat back down with a deep sense of humiliation and tried to figure out their outcome.

They were in a difficult situation now. Having Aurelius as the King's advisor didn't help Eyvind or the others, especially now that he was aware of the broken ties between the father and son. Anything was possible, including death. His mother was his only ally, but she had no powers to wield. His father did not allow her any say in matters of the land.

She was only a figurehead and a mother to the King's sons.

Raidon and Axel were equally stunned to hear that Eyvind had relinquished his claim to the throne. His choice would not only affect them but many others. They were puzzled by his decision and wondered what had precipitated him to do that. Neither could think of a reason that might have driven Eyvind to make a decision of this magnitude. It was almost unheard of for a prince to renounce his inheritance.

Their shoulders slumped as they worried about their own fate and knew they now faced a choice of either serving the King or Eyvind. They didn't know what to expect next as they sat before Audun and his advisor.

"Now which one of you wants to begin? How about you, Raidon? You seem to be the most levelheaded of this bunch," began Aurelius.

Eyvind stayed silent, hunched over while holding his head in his hands. His men had done nothing wrong, and he couldn't figure out what information his father sought from them. It was a known fact, kept secret among the important members of the court, that Aurelius regularly fed into Audun's paranoia, and he, in turn, trusted Aurelius wholly. And it was again paranoia that was driving this bogus interrogation.

"I'm not certain what it is that you are looking for, but all I can tell you is Laris had not quite been himself lately and had been missing for a few days, so we tracked him into the woods where we found him dead," answered Raidon truthfully.

"That simple? And what do you mean 'he wasn't quite himself lately'? Was he sick? You can't possibly expect us to believe that, can you?" protested Aurelius.

Meanwhile, Eyvind became increasingly impatient with Aurelius and just wanted to get the whole thing over with, so he sat upright and began, "I'll tell you everything you need to know. I'm not sure what you're looking for, but hopefully, you will find it and choke on it."

"How dare you! I would mind your loose threats if I were you. Now you are in no position to exert authority over me. You better get used to showing some civility and answering my questions," warned Aurelius, who felt a sense of giddy joy in using his new position of power and authority over Eyvind. Something he couldn't seem to do over the years.

Eyvind huffed in annoyance. He just wanted to deal with this charade quickly and get on with whatever consequences were planned for them. He felt responsible and guilty about dragging Axel and Raidon into this mess and made every attempt to try to insulate them from further persecution. That was why he kept interrupting Aurelius to break his rhythm of questioning.

"A while ago, we were in the forest, on a hunt, when I was charged by a boar that tore through my leg, rendering me incapacitated on the ground…" Eyvind continued with his story, trying to remember as many details as possible.

Both the King and Aurelius were amazed by his tale, and their eyes rounded and nearly popped out of their sockets on hearing about the Imen.

Aurelius rubbed his palms together in glee. He had been in search of such beings with magical powers all his wretched life. This story was a dream come true for him, as now he knew where to go in search of them.

Audun too was left suitably impressed by it and seemed just as excited. This opened so many avenues to beat his enemies easily. Carron would soon be the leader that the other lands most feared.

In all these explanations, there was still an underlying feeling of mistrust toward Eyvind and his fellow Knights, as they didn't offer a satisfactory explanation about Laris' needless murder. How could a woodcutter kill him, and why would he? They were equally suspicious of Eyvind's miraculous injury. All this sounded too good to be true.

At last, Audun pondered and stated, "Only you three knew of this gift that he received from the Imen. Who else would want to kill him for it?"

Raidon stepped forward at this and proceeded with his explanation of how and where they had found Laris and the circumstances surrounding his death.

King Audun shook his head in derision. "Like I said, who would want to kill Laris, especially if he was in a secluded cave well away from the normal path that most townsmen take? Your description doesn't add up. What do you think, Aurelius? Do you agree?"

The advisor agreed with his King. After all, he had a special interest in bringing Eyvind down. "No. It makes no sense at all, Your Highness. Unless... Unless someone knew where he was and tried to ambush him for his prize, perhaps?" His evil eyes cast aspersions on all the soldiers in the group.

Eyvind couldn't believe what he was hearing. Both the King and Aurelius were outright calling him and his men murderers and thieves. "Are you purposing these men... my men...sought him out for the ill-gotten gift that came with a forecast of doom? This is preposterous, and I won't have these honest men accused of such vile acts." His defense came from greater contention but fell on deaf ears.

"If what you say is true...that this miracle took place...then it would be obvious to any reasonable person that Laris lost his trust in the three of you to the point where he refused to be around you lot. He must have stolen away into the forest to escape and plan only to be followed by one of you or perhaps even a spy who snuck up on him and struck him dead, just to steal his gift." Aurelius then turned to his King and asked, "That makes perfect sense to me. How about you, Your Highness?" His voice had the pride of a sleuth who had just solved the greatest mystery of their land.

"You actually think these men, men who are revered by everyone in Carron, would stoop to your cheap methods of spying for a silly cursed trinket?" Disgust was evident in Eyvind's voice.

"Why not? The silly trinket held the potion that could transform things into gold, after all. Isn't that so?" Aurelius countered.

"You disgust me!" Eyvind was losing his patience with the man.

By now, Raidon had had enough and decided to intervene. "Your Majesty, we suspect a certain woodcutter who lives in the forest might be responsible for this atrocious deed because we've run into him several times under strange circumstances, including yesterday morning. His footprints are similar to the ones in the cave, so also the prints of his ox and his cart."

Meanwhile, Axel was itching to defend himself and his friends. Though in such delicate situations, his temperament was not the most ideal, lacking the finesse of diplomacy. The King would certainly not tolerate this. He went on to open his mouth when Raidon, with a shake of his head, forbade him from speaking.

"Oh yes. So you keep saying. Blaming the woodcutter in all this," scoffed King Audun.

"Your Highness, we can track him down and prove to you that he's responsible." Raidon tried his level best to reason with his King.

"Hmm… If you say the woodcutter is responsible for this murder, tell me, how could he know what treasure Laris possessed?" Now King Audun had them in a bind.

"Your Highness, I can't answer this question, but, in all honesty, I can tell you we have a strong suspicion it is him, especially now that we think back on all the encounters we've had with him," replied Raidon.

This caught Audun's interest. "What encounters?"

"Well, we'd caught him spying on us during a hunt where an Imen had appeared and intervened."

"Intervened in what?"

"The Imen...she saved a deer's life...that we hunted." This time, it was Eyvind who answered with annoyance.

"What would possess her to do such a thing? Was it a sacred deer?" mocked Aurelius.

"No, it wasn't," snapped Eyvind.

"Coming back to this woodcutter, what other encounters did you have that piqued your curiosity enough to label him as your main culprit?" Audun interrupted.

"We came across him when he tried to steal gold coins from a man yesterday as we were making our way into the forest in search of Laris," Raidon answered.

"Did you apprehend him? Obviously not, since I can't see him in your custody." Aurelius was completely sarcastic by this point.

"No. Because the man he tried to steal from didn't disclose this truth to us until after the woodcutter had left. We had merely stopped by to ask them if they had seen an Imperial Knight." Raidon tried his utmost to hold on to his patience.

"Do you even hear what you are telling me? The whole thing sounds absurd. Based on these weak encounters, you've solved the mystery surrounding the murder?"

The men refused to answer Aurelius. They could tell this was going nowhere. The King and his advisor had already decided their fate, and this was just a mockery of justice.

After a couple of minutes of silence, Aurelius' attention returned to the Imen, and suddenly Laris' death became meaningless. He began to question them about the mysterious beings. "Getting back to the Imen, where exactly did you say you met them? And, by the way, let me see the injury that you claim to have healed so miraculously," he asked Eyvind who felt thoroughly insulted by this remark.

"Yes. Yes. Let's see this injury of yours," Audun concurred. He motioned Eyvind to raise his pant leg to reveal it.

A deep well of resentment burned within Eyvind, but he complied, pulling up the leg of his pants up to his thigh and exposing the faint scar across his mid-thigh.

King Audun looked at it in complete disbelief. He would have remembered an injury like this, had Eyvind been lying, because it would have taken months to heal. He moved closer and ran a finger along the scar to confirm what he was seeing.

Aurelius too was astounded by this. Hunching over, he took a closer look. Both men looked at one another, each knowing what the other was thinking. They were now consumed by an inexorable frenzy to capture such a magical being that would grant them any victory and fortune they desired.

Both Audun and Aurelius were aware of the consequences that came with such an acquisition. However, they chose to dismiss it as silly superstition even though proof lay before them in the form of the slain Knight. They subtly nodded to each other and stepped away from Eyvind and his men and conferred privately in the corner, then walked toward the group to speak to them.

"Now, about those beings. The Imen? Where did you see them, and what do you know about them?" asked King Audun with deep interest.

The men looked at him and at each other in complete confusion. They had no idea where the Imen came from, and even if they did know, they would rather be hung than disclose the pure beings' location to Audun and Aurelius, whose avarice could be seen on their faces. They realized the King and his advisor were vile men.

Eyvind spoke up, his frustration evident. "We aren't sure where they came from or how they got there. They just appeared out of nowhere and vanished into nowhere. It seemed one second they were there and the next, gone. Poof. Satisfied?"

"You really expect us to believe that? Do you? Especially since the three of you know every square inch of that forest. There is no point in withholding information from me because I'll find out one way or another. You understand?" the King yelled back.

So far, Axel had been quiet, holding his tongue, but now words seemed to burst out of him. "Maybe you should ask the woodcutter since he took the vial from Laris. He must know where the Imen live. After all, he lives in the same forest."

His comment was unexpected, and all his friends were stunned. Even Raidon was unable to restrain him once the words started flowing. But they seemed to work in their favor. He was obviously lying because they had seen the remains of the broken glass vial in the cave.

And, at this point, it didn't matter whether they were lying or telling the truth because it seemed their fates had already been sealed.

Suddenly, Audun and Aurelius were keenly interested in the woodcutter and wanted to know everything about him. They were now convinced they would find out more about the Imen from the woodcutter since he did live there.

After debating for a while, they came to a decision to escort Axel and Raidon into the forest to track down the woodcutter. Eyvind was amazed at how unimportant the foreign diplomats had suddenly become, in the face of magical beings, considering the way his father had hounded him for months about their visit.

Raidon could not leave Eyvind behind, knowing the young Prince's fate lay hanging by a thread. He needed to find a way to convince the King and Aurelius to allow Eyvind to accompany them. He was certain Eyvind would be executed, and going into the forest was his only chance to get away. Together, they could find a way to escape. So, he formulated a plan.

"Your Highness, the Imen who gave Laris the vial befriended Eyvind when she healed him, and she is also the same one who appeared at the deer hunt…on our second encounter. She has taken a liking to him, and I'm certain if Eyvind accompanies us, she is more likely to appear," he reasoned.

Eyvind's eyes narrowed on hearing Raidon's observations and his clever ploy to extract him from a doomed situation. To say he was surprised was an understatement.

Silence rang momentarily until Audun conferred with Aurelius in hushed tones. They were desperate to have an Imen in their hold, and both were willing to risk sending all of them out into the forest. And to prevent their escape, they decided to send well-trained armed guards along with them.

"So be it," said the King benevolently.

"I suppose the visitors have now become unimportant," taunted Eyvind, his voice loaded with sarcasm. "The woodcutter and the Imen have replaced your urgency."

"None of this is any of your concern from now on. I have sent word. Your brother is on his way to complete your job. At least, I know I can count on him," Audun fired back.

"I don't know if I should feel more relief for myself or pity for you."

"Save the pity for yourself. You'll need it when you're hung from the gallows. That's when I'll feel relieved," shouted back Audun, leaving the Imperial Knights shocked and Aurelius rubbing his hands in glee.

"Then you might as well strike me down now and get it over with. I won't resist you," Eyvind replied in defiance.

Aurelius hoped the King would do just that and get rid of the spoke in his plans. But the King replied calmly, "Believe me, I would. But first, I need that Imen girl. See, you're not completely worthless. You still hold some temporary value for Carron."

Eyvind was disgusted by his father and spat on the ground. His father's words had ended the tenuous bond between them.

"Get them out of here and on their way!"

Those were the last words he heard from his father as he was herded out by Aurelius' men.

QUEEN TARA OF CARTHINIA paced the spacious guest quarters of Carron. King Camden watched her tense and rigid figure move back and forth like the limbs of a barren tree blown by a wicked wind. That means she was plotting, and it made him uneasy.

Tara was deep in thought and unaware of the King's gaze upon her. She was annoyed at having to wait for the spies whom she had sent to gather information to come back with a report. She was, after all, the driving force behind King Camden and his empire.

The eldest of nine, born into extreme poverty, her parents had sold her off as a servant to a wealthy nobleman and his wife at a very young age. Having no children of their own, they treated her with kindness, generosity, and love despite her lowly status.

Tara was not a beauty by any measure; however, she was petite and fair-skinned with long brown hair and hypnotic dark eyes like those of a snake.

From the very beginning, Tara resented being born into poverty and coveted a life of grandeur. After seeing how the nobleman and his wife lived, she knew she was made for that life and concealed the disdain and envy she held against them. As she grew older, this hatred had carved a deep chasm in her, one that demanded to be avenged.

The nobleman and his wife were unaware of Tara's hidden contempt, and as far as they were concerned, she was happy with her lot in life. There was nary a doubt in them that she was so resentful of their wealth and status. Tara too performed her duties flawlessly, always careful to never cast suspicion upon herself. She was, in reality, a vile creature but a superb actress.

Over time, her conduct in their home became more brazen. She would wait until the mistress left the house and then instantly rush to her boudoir to don the fine gowns and jewelry. She loved seeing herself adorned in gold and precious gems.

Being the wicked creature that she was, she fantasized about different scenarios in front of the mirror, thrusting herself into another world where she was the mistress and had dozens of servants to order. She would do this regularly, dream up different fantasies, until she heard the horses draw the carriage up to the house. Only then would she scuttle to change back into her own clothes.

"If only I could wake up from his dreadful nightmare someday and find myself a Prince," she would lament to herself in mounting frustration. The insane desire for power and wealth drove her mad, and as time passed, this urge grew exponentially.

Tara had sworn a vow to herself to overcome all obstacles and become a woman of notoriety. She patiently awaited that day and spent every spare moment thinking about how to transform her desires and wishes into reality. From that day on, she was obsessed.

She saved as much money as she could, but each month she received pleading letters from her family asking for more. One afternoon, after resentfully sending off almost all of her wages to her family, she sat in her austere room with one bed and a threadbare rug, staring at her plain surroundings in complete frustration. That was the day she made an absolute resolution to put an end to her lowly status as a chambermaid forever. She would do whatever it took, by hook or crook, to marry into nobility and enter the highest status of the land.

A servant marrying into royalty was unheard of and presented a great hurdle for her to overcome, making her uncertain of how to achieve that goal. All she had with her was her cunningness, determination, and uncanny ability to control and sway the minds of people around her. And she used this ability to force others to believe that her parents were of noble birth, had given away the firstborn, which was her, as a servant at the directions of a priest in order to have a male child born into the family to carry on the family name.

Although only a few believed her, they still went along with her story out of fear.

Tara made up wicked lies about those who didn't go along with her tales and had them sacked. It was not for nothing that she had the blind trust of her masters, who did as she instructed. She spread fabricated gossip and rumors about others to maintain an environment of distrust and chaos at all times. Her simple reasoning in all this was—if no one got along with one another, it would be difficult for them to get together to plot against her. An excellent idea that worked for years.

Surprisingly, none of this had been apparent to her masters, who in fact viewed her as a valuable member of their staff, believing her to be sweet, dedicated, and someone who looked out for their best interests. Little did they know how cold, calculating, and nefarious a creature she could be, who only looked out to serve her selfish interests at the expense of others. No one dared to challenge her out of fear of severe repercussions. Times were tough, and they needed their jobs.

Years passed, and Tara grew older. Looking into the mirror and seeing the tiny lines at the angles of her eyes, she realized she had to work fast. Time was not on her side. She became so frustrated that she began to contemplate murder. Murder of the nobleman and his wife. Each time she saw her mistress, it grated on her because she was reminded of her own lowly status. And that sickened her, and all her schemes were to no avail. She secretly wished ill will upon both.

Yet, their love and compassion for Tara never diminished. They had been simply ignorant about the wickedness that brewed behind her flat dark eyes, and that suited her well.

Soon her murderous plot slowly took shape in her mind. All she needed was a moment to her advantage. And she got it.

One day, her mistress announced they were going to hold a grand gala at the estate, and amongst those invited, it was none other than the King himself.

King Camden was a young bachelor who had recently been crowned after his elder brother had unexpectedly died in an accident during a pachyderm hunt.

Camden was unlike his charismatic brother, who had been clever, self-assured, and powerful. Camden had spent most of his life living in his brother's shadow. Insecure and unsure of his own decisions, he possessed none of his brother's qualities.

The Queen Mother had initially not been keen on having her nation reigned by a King who didn't possess the confidence to rule. But she had no choice because the only other person to inherit the throne was her daughter Princess Ania, who was much too young for this task. Hence, Camden was proclaimed the King of Carthinia.

Tara knew the grand ball was the chance she was seeking. She had one great opportunity to achieve her goal.

"There's hope for me," Tara cried out in a frenzied but hushed tone.

Although not stunningly beautiful, she had an uncanny ability to quickly assess the shortcomings of others and use them to her advantage. She prided herself on possessing this cunning prowess that helped her to control others.

In her mind, she viewed herself as an irresistible creature and did everything to drive that image into everyone's head with brutal force. Silently, she dared anyone to disagree, and no one ever did, at least not to her face.

From the moment she heard the news about the gala, she was obsessed and scrambled to formulate the steps of her plot. This was an opportunity that would come along only once in her lifetime. She needed to make a foolproof plan that was well thought out and carried out flawlessly.

First, she needed a gown, not just any gown but something that would blow everyone's minds and show off her figure perfectly. Frantically rummaging through her mistress' trunks in the attic, where the old gowns were stashed, Tara began to rifle through box after box in haste and with mounting fury until she found something suitable. It was an elegant gown that her mistress had worn once to a very special occasion. Tara's wicked little hands were all over it, caressing the fabric with love. She could see her plan becoming successful. She held it against her body and rushed to the dusty mirror, stashed away in the dim corner of the attic, and swaying in front of it for a moment, she imagined herself in the arms of King Camden.

The gown was much too long for her small stature and ill-fitting, but that didn't worry her much. She was determined to get it shortened and modified in time for the gala, even if she had to sit up nights to do it.

Tara filched the gown from the attic and worked on it feverishly to alter it in time.

Stealing from the employers who had treated her well was of no consequence to her. In her mind, she was borrowing it and besides, they owed her for the years of her service to them.

A reprehensible act devoid of conscience was this that revealed her true nature, but there was no one to see her evil at the moment. The extent of her treachery and depravity would come to light much later when it was too late.

She was meticulous in her planning and gathered all the information she could about the King. Never could it be said that Tara did not do her homework on those who were in the crosshairs of her sight.

At long last the day she had been feverishly waiting for had arrived. But she still hadn't given the finishing touches to her gown, and the last bit of hemming was still pending. She rushed all day, tending to her tasks, and snuck away to work on her gown at any possible chance.

Even her mistress noticed Tara's strange behavior. However, she was too busy overseeing the particulars of the grand affair to pay her much attention.

There were many smaller details that needed careful consideration, and just when Tara thought she was done, her mistress burdened her with more tasks. Finally, out of frustration, Tara abandoned all her duties and stole away to prepare for the evening.

As she began dressing, she rehearsed in her mind the script of the lines she would say to the King—determined beyond all odds to accomplish what she had vowed to do. This was her one and only chance in life to attain all that she wanted.

That evening, the guests started trickling in, and it wasn't long before the horns and trumpets blasted to alert everyone of the arrival of the royals.

Tara put on the finishing touches to her gown but still needed time to make it shine to perfection. She cursed and threw things across the room in complete exasperation as she frantically completed the alterations and got dressed.

She draped the gown around her body, and the fabric settled upon her skin like soft petals where its skirt pooled about her in layers of cascading chiffon. The upward scooping corset revealed her smooth shoulders and accentuated her neck. It was an outfit that showed off the best part of her while leaving little to the imagination. Looking at herself in the mirror, she caressed the silk of her gown and nodded with approval.

"Today, you'll emerge as the Queen. And no one can stop your plans," she whispered with absolute conviction as she turned and departed her austere chamber. Sophisticated and polished like no one had ever seen her to be.

Tara hurried to the festivities as fast as she could, stopping just before the grand hall. She slowed her pace as she approached the hall and caught her breath. She noticed her master and mistress receiving the King and knew this was her opportunity to needle her way in.

As she pushed through the dignitaries, the other staff noticed and recognized her. "Tara?" they remarked in one voice and, as always, got back a look that spoke volumes of her wrath. They maintained their silence, fearing her fury.

Tara pushed through and took a position next to her master and mistress.

They were shocked to see her dressed like that and wondered what she was doing next to them, but it was neither the time nor the place to ask her questions since the King was standing before them.

"Welcome, Your Majesty. It's an honor to have you here." Her master greeted the King with a polite smile and introduced his wife.

Tara too had planned everything perfectly. Just at the right moment, when the King glanced briefly at her, she had the audacity to introduce herself as the orphan niece to her masters, who were both astonished by her brazen behavior.

What is she up to? And why is she dressed like that? Her mistress thought, looking at her husband, wondering if he was the one who had invited her to join them.

Being from the polite upper society, they had to hold their tongue and not make a fuss right there. Tara knew that and took undue advantage of the situation. She gave them no opportunity to question her for the remainder of the evening, standing close to the King's side at all times, as if riveted by his conversations.

The festivities went on, and Tara stayed glued by Camden's side, showering him with accolades and words of admiration. She had done her research well and had discovered the

King lacked self-confidence, and the constant comparison with his brother had made him insecure. She knew exactly how to captivate him for the rest of the night. She stroked his ego, spoke the right words, payed rich compliments continuously, making him the focus of her attention. Camden loved the attention, and he was hooked.

By the end of the evening, he was completely oblivious to everyone around him and felt secure and confident like never before, when she was by his side. Tara's words had done their magic, and she had grown on him, never realizing that her compliments lacked sincerity and only served an ulterior motive. This marked the beginning of their courtship…

When Tara finally became the queen, she took immediate steps to take care of all the loose ends. Her former master and mistress were killed by her secret spies, and the remaining staff too were silenced forever. There was nobody to utter a word and reveal her true identity.

Despite all her thorough efforts, whispers about her got out, and she was not well-liked. Many were aware of her malicious intentions and called her the "Pauper Queen."

After silencing her employers, she moved her family into their grand estate and secretly gave them money on a regular basis. They were under strict instructions to never hint at their relationship or utter a word about it, under the threat that they would stop receiving money.

They gladly complied as they were all cut from the same cloth, just as depraved and devoid of scruples as she was.

Shortly after marrying Camden, she became his closest and strict advisor on every matter. And he too sought her opinion on each of his decisions. Tara was not only his wife but also his highest confidant.

The Queen Mother and Ania, Camden's sister, were not keen on his continued dependence on Tara for every decision. Ania was a gentle soul with a sweet temperament, and for the most part, she kept to herself and stayed as far away from Tara as possible.

Aware of Tara's wicked motives and the control she wielded over her brother, Ania maintained her silence for the sake of diplomacy. She knew more about Tara than she could have imagined. The Queen Mother, due to her failing health, realized she would not live much longer and wanted all the royal jewels that were in her safekeeping to be passed down to Ania and not Tara.

Tara had not become the Queen by being naïve. She desperately wanted every last piece and was not going to let anything stop her. As the Queen Mother's physical health deteriorated so did her mental health. She lapsed into a state of confusion and delirium, which presented a great opportunity for Tara to pilfer the jewels from the dying woman.

She drew up an official document, stating the jewels were to be bequeathed to her and had the Queen Mother sign it whilst in a state of mental impairment. Ania was, of course, unaware of this underhanded interaction.

Upon the Queen Mother's death, Tara promptly produced the document, presented it to Camden, and took possession of all the items, leaving Ania in a state of outrage. But, at this point, there was nothing much Ania could do since she had no other ally left. Her mother was her only support, and she was gone. Ania was grief-struck on seeing Tara's dirty dealings and became gravely ill, wishing she too were dead.

Camden was concerned about his sister's health but remained completely oblivious to what was happening around him. He never ever came to know, to this day, that it was Tara's unscrupulous acts that were the cause of his sister's failing health. Ania, on her part, maintained her silence and continued to languish in mental agony.

One day, Tara paid her a visit, and instead of offering solace to the innocent soul, she tortured Ania with cruel barbs that were meant to hurt her right to her core. Stressing on her own superiority and tormenting Ania about her so-called "inferiority," Tara showed no mercy or compassion for the dying girl, who was already sick with grief. Tara kept emphasizing on Ania's weakness and pelted her with sadistic statements almost continually, forcing her to accept she was a weak and inferior creature who would amount to nothing.

Ania was very attractive, and it was obvious that she presented a threat to Tara, who was completely intolerant of anyone prettier than her. Tara was like a snake, and by using her hypnotic eyes and forked tongue, she could easily brainwash others into believing that they weren't as attractive as her.

Ania had been a tough nut to crack. She refused to believe or acknowledge anything Tara told her even as she lay on her deathbed. Unable to tolerate the blank expression on Ania's face and wanting to destroy her completely, a wrathful demon awakened within Tara as she stormed out to instruct her chambermaid to give the dying girl a drink to which she furtively added poison. The chambermaid unwittingly served that drink to Ania.

Tara waited a while and then returned to Ania's chamber just in time to watch the last breath escape from the girl's sweet lips. She sat back in great satisfaction, congratulating herself silently on having removed the last obstacle from her life. Looking at the smooth visage of the dead girl, Tara admired her nefarious deed with a rush of pleasure as though the dead girl was a work of art.

Cruel. Unkind. Calculating. She was all this and more. After concluding the ugly deed, she pinched herself hard and whipped up tears, then tore off to inform Camden of the bad news.

He was devastated on hearing about his sister's death as Tara convinced him that she had been by Ania's side all through the day, holding her hand and consoling her until her last breath.

He was touched by his wife's devotion and had no reason to doubt her. After all, she had helped him with everything. He could not have amassed so much wealth and power had it not been for Tara's suggestions of higher taxation and confiscation of properties. Little did he know, nor did he bother to find out, that the people of his land had been barely getting by prior to the burden of increased taxes. All pleas to the King regarding their hardship had been intercepted and denied by Tara.

There was now an undercurrent of discontent that brewed in the masses as Tara continued using intimidation and duress to keep things at bay. But she was not astute enough to recognize such tactics caused seeds of uprising to germinate.

As years passed, Tara gave birth to their daughter Adina, but she did not have many of those maternal feelings to shower the child with love. She took advantage of every opportunity that came her way. Even the motive behind this union for Carthinia via marriage was to learn the layout of Jasper so they could mount a surprise attack on it and conquer this land full of natural resources, riches, and luxuries. This would be the first time they would get the greatest opportunity to defeat their sworn enemy once and for all. Tara had decided she would not rest until Carthinian flags flew from the highest masts over Jasper. It was ironic that both sides were busy spinning treacherous webs to meet their own greedy objectives.

"Where are they? I'll have their heads on a spit if they don't return with useful information," Tara muttered as she nervously paced back and forth the room.

"Will you stop pacing? You're making me nervous. I'm not too keen on being here. It's enemy territory, after all, and sending out spies right away on the first night…it…it's not the right way to go about these things," remarked Camden as she watched his wife's taut frame.

"Then what do you suggest? We take up residence for a month until we get adjusted? We're here for a very short time, and I'm going to dig up as much information as possible about these people because I intend to return with an army to take over their land and all their riches. Carthinia will conquer Carron. You mark my words, Camden."

Camden was exhausted from the journey and all the following events, and his mind was set on taking a nap. He sighed loud enough to draw his wife's attention toward it. In a typical Tara fashion, she rolled her eyes in frustration but continued pacing.

"I know they're up to something. This whole peace thing is a charade. It just doesn't sit well…never has. Do they think we're really that stupid? They've sadly underestimated me," she laughed, knowing she had some shocks up her sleeve.

Camden knew it was useless arguing with her as she was usually right and always managed to carry out whatever she set out to do. But, he wasn't fully aware of the extent of her cruelty in getting things done.

However, he knew many things that she thought she had concealed well enough from him. But being a circumspect husband, he chose to maintain his ignorance about them.

His introspection and her pacing were abruptly halted by a soft knock on the door. Before anyone else could know, Tara rushed into the adjoining living area to see who it was.

She refused to have any servants around when she had matters of secrecy to discuss— she trusted no one. When confidentiality was needed, she would revert to her previous lowly status and perform many of the tasks herself unlike a royal queen or a lady of high stature.

At long last, they were here, the ones she had been waiting for.

"In here," she instructed, exasperation loaded in her tone.

The leader of the spies followed her into her chamber, where she questioned him about every detail and threatened him multiple times when he hesitated while answering. He also provided various diagrams while Tara also made additional detailed ones of everything that was being reported to her. She went over and over all of them multiple times to make sure he wasn't making up or forgetting any of the smaller details.

He gave her all the information, but she seemed dissatisfied, nonetheless. After grilling him tons of times, asking the same questions in different ways and making him go through all the diagrams, just to ensure he wasn't withholding any information, she finally let him leave. The leader let out a huge sigh of relief as he departed from the chamber. The rest of the staff and his own team of spies—aware of the duress Tara placed him under—sympathized with him secretly.

As he exited the chamber, Adina entered and wished to see her parents.

She knocked on their door and heard her mother bark out from within, "What is it now?"

Adina feared her mother much more than her father.

Tara's tone indicated it might not be a good time to approach her on any matters that would cause much consternation. Adina stood frozen, uncertain, and debated with herself whether she should enter the chamber.

"Who is it?" Tara yelled out again impatiently.

Trembles ran down Adina's spine, and caught in a quandary, she quickly came to a decision. Before she could execute it, the door flew open, and her mother stood before her, ready to bark out at her one more time.

"Oh, it's you. What is it now?" Tara asked, motioning her in.

Adina timidly entered the chamber and rushed to hug her father. Tara despised Camden's relationship with Adina. The wretched creature that she was, Tara was always jealous of her and barely tolerated her for the sake of maintaining her position. She had no qualms about sacrificing Adina for her own greed. Her daughter was just a pawn in her never-ending game and struggle for more power and wealth.

On the other hand, Adina was everything her mother was not: sweet, naïve, and a hopeless romantic. Someone who lacked her mother's cutthroat nature. Raised by her paternal grandmother and aunt, she had taken on their qualities, especially their kindness.

Tara did not appreciate her daughter's gentle nature and perceived it as a weakness, which Adina was quite aware of. Her mother was not the sort to keep such things to herself.

"Homesick already?" Tara asked her coldly.

"No, Mother..." she replied nervously, fearful about saying anything more.

Her hesitation made Tara all the more irritated. She despised weakness in all forms. And Adina was clearly displaying it by cowering in front of her.

"Stop acting so nervous. It's not becoming of a Princess. What is it?"

Adina looked at her father, hoping for support before she spoke, which he didn't fail to give her.

"What's the matter, child?" he asked lovingly.

Adina timidly began. "It's about this marriage arrangement."

"What about it?" interrupted her mother.

"Well..."

"Well, what?" Tara's voice rose with every word.

"Will you please give the girl a chance? Must you always jump down everyone's throat? Let her speak. You're making her nervous. Can't you see?" Camden turned toward his daughter. "Now, what is it, Adina?"

Tara resented being chastised by Camden before their daughter and wanted to lash out at both of them. However, at the moment, she needed Camden's cooperation to fulfill certain parts of her plan before taking the liberty to discard him as well. He was becoming a millstone around her neck.

Although the citizens of Carthinia were not pleased with the hardship rules and the stringent laws imposed upon them, they knew Tara was the driving force behind it, not their king. The discontented insurgence had remained forgiving of Camden thus far.

However, there was no telling how long he would enjoy their benevolence until they too turned on him. A factor Tara was aware of to some extent.

Hiding her growing bitterness, she held her tongue and painfully wondered what the silly girl was going to complain about.

"It's about Eyvind," Adina explained.

Tara brewed in silence, restraining herself from lashing out at her. She hoped Adina had not fouled this plan or the union because she needed this marriage to happen at all costs. There was no turning back.

"Go on," encouraged Camden.

"I've never told this to either of you in the past, but I'm in love with someone else—" she stated before she was immediately interrupted by her mother.

"In love? What are you talking about? With whom?" screamed Tara, breaking her decision to be silent. She was furious. This stupid girl was ruining her plans.

"Will you please…?" Camden pleaded without completing the line. He wanted to hear what his daughter had to say.

"I'm in love with Eyvind's brother, Korin," Adina confessed.

Camden and Tara were speechless. *How could that be? Where could she have met him? They had been so careful.* A thousand more questions rang in their heads. They both questioned Adina in depth and were more shocked to hear Korin had been entering Carthinia and perhaps spying on them. This made the royal couple wonder just what the Carronites were up to.

Tara immediately seized the opportunity to defend her action of sending spies to memorize and map out the layout of the castle and the different areas in Jasper.

She started ranting angrily, "I told you, Camden, these people are not to be trusted. They've been spying on us the entire time." She felt vindicated.

Adina remained oblivious to her mother's outbursts. Spies and wars were not something she was ever interested in. Her sole aim in speaking to her parents had been to decline the offer to marry Eyvind and hope they would understand her dilemma.

But now thoughts were pouring into her mind as she realized this union had nothing to do with its original intent. She was realizing she had just been a pawn in an insane game of perpetual war and dominance. Suddenly, she worried about her own fate. The reality of being forced to marry Eyvind loomed in her head.

"Stupid girl! You have ruined it all. How could you be so ignorant and not know who he was?" her mother chastised her.

"Neither of us was honest with the other," she countered Tara scornfully.

"Of course, only you would think that is what is most important. Where did you first meet him? When did you meet him? I need to know everything. You will not leave this room until you reveal the smallest details about your encounters."

Adina was horrified as each question put forth by her mother tightened the noose around her neck. She was scared to death of her mother.

"Well…?" Tara yelled.

Adina nervously proceeded to tell them both about all her rendezvous with Rin, defending her actions by claiming she had no way of knowing who he really was. When she was done, her justifications brought Tara down on her hard.

"Silence! You have done enough damage here, to jeopardize all my plans. It's hard to believe you were borne by me. You probably didn't even think to ask him where he was from. Did you?" Tara snapped at her daughter in disgust and disappointment.

"I'm sorry, Mother, but it's not as though I planned this or knew who he was. He also doesn't know who I am," she offered.

"Only a foolish girl like you would take anything said to her at face value without being the least bit inquisitive. Only you!" She cast her blame on Adina as she paced across the room in fury.

"Enough! I won't have you berating her in this manner," interjected Camden.

"And I won't have this plan abandoned because she's in love with his brother. Tough! That's all I have to say in this matter. You'll marry Eyvind, and that's final! What you do with his brother...whatever his name is...is up to you," dictated Tara, laying down her terms.

Now it was Camden who was put in a difficult position. He was in a conundrum and gave the situation serious consideration but came up empty.

Meanwhile, Tara shot piercing glares at him that made her position clear.

In the end, he was forced to concede and give his decision. "Look here, Adina, this matter had been decided and arranged for a while, and you went along with it. Unfortunately for you, Korin happens to be Eyvind's brother. I'm sorry, but this union will have to continue as planned. It would be catastrophic for us if we break this alliance," he replied regretfully.

Mortified by his statement, Adina felt abandoned by her only ally. Alone and having nothing else to say, she ran out of the chamber in tears.

Tara was pleased with Camden's handling of the situation and especially for supporting her stance. But she worried Adina might do something stupid, so she sent a soldier to follow and keep an eye on her in case she tried to kill herself or worse, divulge their plans to Eyvind. Tara was convinced everyone was as spiteful and conniving as she.

"She certainly doesn't take after me," stated Tara as she poured a glass of wine and gulped it down in one go.

Camden was torn by the predicament Adina was facing, but it had to be this way for now because too much was at stake.

"Let me have one," he asked of her in a melancholic tone as he then sat back with his glass, numbly dwelling on what had just transpired.

IT DIDN'T TAKE BUT a flash for Bomo to reach his lair. Rushing in haste, he slammed the door shut and barricaded it with various pieces of furniture as he strode deeper into his dusty, unkempt abode, progressively blocking and securing each room with furniture. He checked and assured himself before going forward in the direction of his study.

Upon reaching it, he carefully pulled out the Lightning rose and placed it on the table in front of him. The freakish creature drew a chair back and sat down to stare at it from afar. He was speechless.

His massive brow furrowed, pointing at the bridge of his nose, and his eyes seemed to glow with an unholy fervor as he stared at the most precious thing set before him. He never thought he could ever have a Lightning Rose in his possession.

"I 'ave you now. You're mine!" He whispered to himself as he sat snickering proudly upon his rickety chair.

After happily patting himself on his back for a job well done, he decided to get on with his business. The Lightning Rose was just one of the ingredients. Now he had to get his spell ready, so he sprang into action and gathered the rest of the items needed for it. Busy following the steps listed in his mother's book, he lit a big fire and set his cauldron upon it. Then he proceeded to again read the instructions carefully before placing every single one of them into the cauldron.

He wanted to make sure to not miss a single step or ingredient. This was his only chance because he might never find another Lightning Rose again. So he couldn't afford to bungle this once-in-a-lifetime opportunity.

Aside from a lone, small torch that was burning in one corner of the room, the main source of light came from the fire beneath the cauldron. Bomo hovered over it with his big mouth agape as his fiendish eyes peered into it, imagining how he would capture Roni. Evil glee and malice shone from his eyes.

The fire cast an ominous shadow of his body upon the stone wall, making him appear twice as menacing. His laughter reverberated in the four walls of his study. When done with the last item, he proceeded to add the final and the most important ingredient—the Lightning Rose.

He carefully plucked the petals from the flower and added them one by one into the disgusting brew. His pea-sized brain worked harder, thinking about all the things he would do once he captured Roni. Insane with happiness, he stirred the contents with brute force.

"Roni… Roni… Roni…"

He repeated her name over and over… almost like a fervent prayer.

Once done, he carefully stowed away the concoction in a sealed glass vial and exited from his chamber.

He removed the barricades from every room as he crossed it and cautiously creaked open the front door of his slovenly abode. Just wide enough to allow his yellowish eyes to peek out and check if the coast was clear. He saw no movement anywhere. Everything was the same as before when he had arrived home, and not a single bough or leaf moved.

He opened the door further and stepped out, craning his thick neck in all directions to check his surroundings for intruders. And he wasn't satisfied until he had walked the perimeter of his property twice.

He returned to his house and bolted the door shut behind him, then hurried to his study. Fetching the ornate box in which he had placed the teardrop-shaped glass vial, he strained his brain hard to think about how to cast the spell on Roni or where he could find her.

The book just stated that anyone who came in contact with the concoction would be affected by it.

Should I just throw it at her? No...no...too risky.

Roni moved too fast for him to catch her. He considered luring her into a trap but had no clue how to accomplish that.

After pondering it from all angles, and in consternation, he came up with a clever idea of transferring some of the potion into a fragile glass bottle and hit her with it using a slingshot. He could do this from a distance and not worry about her fleeing fast. She wouldn't know what had hit her until it did.

Besides, the slingshot was the only weapon in his arsenal. He was so proud of himself for thinking up such a clever idea that he danced clumsily all around the room and almost fell over the upturned books on the floor. He caught himself in time because had he fallen, the precious liquid in his hand would have smashed into pieces, and he would have fallen victim to his own spell.

The maladroit ogre's heart pounded hard and fast at his near blunder. Sweating profusely, he took deep breaths and steadied himself. He regained his awkward composure while searching his study for tiny, fragile vials until he found some stashed away deep in a drawer.

Bomo then began the task of breaking the seal from around the teardrop vial and transferring the strange content into two fragile vials which he sealed with wax as before. He saved some of the original liquid for future use, resealing the teardrop bottle carefully and returning it in its ornate box on the high shelf. Next, he placed the tiny vials in a leather pouch that he slung across his chest and moved on to the next task—the search for his slingshot.

Once he found it, he clutched it in his hand tightly and slammed the main door shut behind him, then locked it with a big, well-worn key. He checked around for a final time to make sure there was no danger surrounding him and then set out on his mission.

He plodded through the forest, searching everywhere for Roni. Hours passed, and there was no sign of anyone. The clod made up his mind to not return home until he succeeded in his task.

The threat of the Imperial Knights coming after him for murder was out of sight and out of mind for the simpleton. His only concern was to find and capture the jewel of the forest.

As the day lingered on with orange streaks in the sky, Bomo's tiny little brain wandered off to other things, and his attention became distracted. He instinctively surveyed trees for future chopping, calculating how many cartloads and gold coins they would fetch.

He kept losing focus on his mission as his thoughts continued to slip away onto different matters. It wasn't long before he found himself surveying a large tree for future chopping. But then suddenly, he saw a figure moving through the forest at a distance.

Seized with eagerness, Bomo wondered who it was and if it were she. The ogre hurried in the same direction, and as he got closer, he saw the figure clearly. He still wasn't certain who it was because the person looked like a soldier.

Bomo immediately fell to his knees and ducked low in case it was the Imperial Knight looking for him. He continued to monitor him and, upon closer examination, realized he had never seen a uniform such as the one this soldier wore. He wondered where the person was from.

Who's ee? Where'd ee come from? He questioned his brain, hoping for an answer.

Bomo was curious about this strange person and decided to follow him to see what he was up to.

Maybe it's the Prince!

His heart pounded hard at the possibility, both in excitement and fear. He felt the Prince might have a way of luring Roni, and if so, he would strike them both with the potion and turn them into pebbles.

He would take Roni but discard the Prince. He was so proud of his intelligence and brilliant ways of thinking up fantastic strategies.

Leaping forth, he moved stealthily through the forest, maintaining a good distance between himself and the stranger.

He noticed the "Prince" was searching the ground for something.

Wot's ee lookin' for? He grimaced when he stumbled across a tree root. Picking up his pace, he moved closer to see if he could hear anything. Eventually, he heard whispered words.

"White flower trail? I wonder where it is. Got to be here somewhere."

White flower trail? Wot's that? He pondered again, with no reply from his cranium.

He waited and watched the "Prince" move about, eyes focused on the ground, as he combed the forest floor.

Bomo continued to observe him carefully, but then something occurred to him. The voice! The tone! There was something vaguely familiar about it. The clod moved closer to get a better listen.

He stretched his ear with his fat fingers in the direction of the individual and waited. Looking very silly doing this, he followed the figure through the woods and waited to hear the voice again.

The figure continued to search the ground and then suddenly stopped and surveyed in all directions.

Bomo too came to an abrupt stop and hid behind a large boulder.

It seemed that the "Prince" had found whatever he sought because he proceeded to remove the helmet from his head and nod in satisfaction.

Upon removing the helmet, Bomo noticed that the person was not the Prince but instead was a woman.

As she turned around to examine her surroundings, he saw her face.

Bomo was seized by waves of exhilaration. *It was her! Roni!* He was in a state of rapture and could hardly control himself or his awkward body.

He flailed around and made a tremendous ruckus, alerting Roni, who was startled by the noise.

She paused for a split second and looked around to see where the sounds were emanating from. At a distance, she saw a large, klutzy creature thrashing about, which frightened her. Never had she come across someone like Bomo.

Realizing what her parents had told her, she put her helmet back on and ran through the forest to get away from the creature.

Looking down, she found the white flower trail. It had been right there the whole time. The flowers were sporadic, but if one looked carefully, they showed a clear path. It was almost as if someone had dropped tiny white indicators to mark the trail. There it was, as her parents had said—a clear white trail.

Roni made a run for it, not knowing who the creature behind was or what he wanted.

ENJI PLEADED WITH SUKI, "We must go up and accompany her."

"I'm not sure that's a good idea, Kenji. What if we get caught? I'm certain it's forbidden," rebutted Suki.

"No one told us we couldn't. Can you recall such a law?" he reasoned, desperation lining his words.

Suki thought hard but couldn't think of anything off the top of her head, so apprehensively agreed to come along.

Pleased at convincing her, Kenji hurried her to an exit from where they quickly emerged in the forest.

They both looked around to see if Roni was anywhere in sight but saw no traces of her. They searched around for clues, trying to decipher the chamber from where she was dispelled, as that would give them an indication of her position in relation to them. Wild guesses served them no purpose.

Finally, Kenji decided to whisper out her name.

"Roni... Roni... Roni..."

Both waited, hoping for some reply back. Alas, they found no sign of her.

They combed the forest aimlessly, expecting to run into her, but she was nowhere to be found. After a while, they both sat down on a bright rock, ready to concede defeat. Only one thought swirled in their minds.

Where is Roni sent? What will become of her?

They knew most of the forest, having been here all their lives; however, they were dumbfounded when they found no tracks of her. Not a shadow of her whereabouts could be seen or heard, and both of them were good trackers.

"I think we better get back, Kenji. We're already too far from where we're supposed to be. This isn't good. Away from the center of the forest, there are no Boad trees around here for us to go back home," Suki observed fearfully, taking in the sight around them.

Kenji was torn because part of him wanted to return home before they got into serious trouble, yet the other half that was loyal to Roni wanted to stay and help his friend get to her destination safely even though he had no idea where her destination lay.

Suki tugged at Kenji gently to get him to leave, and eventually, he complied.

As they began to make their way back, they were startled by a strange sound heard at a distance. They ducked behind a large tree and waited.

"What's that noise?" Suki's voice quivered in fear.

"I don't know." Kenji carefully peeked from behind the tree to see if he could get a better look at what or who could be making the sound. He saw nothing.

However, he could still hear the commotion, and it was getting closer. They both ducked low within the shrubs and hid in the shadows until the source of the ruckus came into view. Kenji managed to get his first sight of the ogre.

It was a barbaric-looking specimen, with a huge head and golden-yellow eyes, lumbering through the forest with an awkward gait, droning an incoherent chant repeatedly. In his hands, he held a slingshot while a leather strap hung diagonally across his chest with a pouch resting at his hip. The creature walked in their direction, then stopped.

Silence fell upon the forest all of a sudden.

"What happened?" Suki whispered in Kenji's ear nervously.

Her friend held out his hand to calm her and peeked again to see what was happening but saw nothing. The being had disappeared.

"Kenji! Who's he?" Suki's nervousness could no longer be hidden.

"I don't know. I don't see or hear it anymore," he replied as he craned his neck to get a better look.

There wasn't a thing in sight.

He crouched back down and remained there. He could have slowed time to see what was going on, but because they weren't supposed to be snooping in the first place, they both felt they too might face uncertain consequences, so they remained hidden in their places.

They listened carefully for any sound, but none could be heard.

"I wonder where he went?" Kenji whispered as he took another glance.

"Who was he?" asked Suki, who was clearly frightened.

"Some strange-looking creature," he replied, not knowing how to describe the specimen in a way she wouldn't get more scared.

"Creature?" she asked with anxiety.

"Don't know how else to describe it," he replied.

"In that case, we better return home before we get into a lot of trouble. I don't think I want to be banished to this place with creatures like the one you just saw," she said.

Kenji understood Suki's apprehension and didn't want to cause her any more distress, so he complied.

They began to head home, but they hadn't gone more than a few steps when they heard a name echo through the forest ahead of them. A name that they knew.

"Roni, Roni, Roni. Yes, my Roni."

"That's Roni's name. Did you hear that?" Suki's fear escalated as she clutched Kenji's arm in a deathly grip.

"Yes, I did," Kenji answered as he stared in the direction from where the chant originated.

"How does he know Roni?" Suki asked fearfully.

"I don't know, and that's a good question." Kenji was certain this was not the hunter whom Roni had helped that first day and who was now the cause of her banishment. This was clearly someone with ill intent in his heart.

Kenji stealthily moved through the forest to find the creature, with Suki following close at his heels.

Every few steps they paused to check if they could hear any more sounds. Nothing was heard for some distance, but eventually, reverberations of a crazed rant reached their ears. But it was hard to discern what was being said.

The pair hunkered low and swiftly moved in the direction of the sound.

At last, they caught sight of the specimen. A gasp left Suki's mouth when she beheld the scene before her. An out-of-proportion, hideous creature, the likes she had never seen before was in front of her, tugging his ear as if trying to listen for something.

How can this creature know Roni?

The common thought struck their minds.

The ogre pushed his way through the thick vegetation and seemed to be in pursuit of someone, which made them both very anxious.

Is it Roni?

They followed him silently, keeping pace with him as close as they could while staying inconspicuous. They didn't know if the creature had sharp hearing.

"You think he's chasing Roni?" Suki asked in a whisper, her voice barely audible in the noise the ogre was making.

"He might be," Kenji whispered back.

An expression of concern clouded their eyes, and worry marred their foreheads. They had to find Roni before the creature did. They didn't know what this being wanted from Roni but were certain it could be nothing good. A sense of urgency swept over them to find their friend and alert her. They scanned the area around them but could see no signs of her.

It was getting late, and Suki and Kenji had veered far away from home. Others at Imen-Hera would surely be missing them. After a short debate of heated whispers, they decided to continue to look for Roni a little while longer. They couldn't possibly let her fall prey to this madman.

With the ungainly specimen halting in his tracks in front of them and no longer tugging at his ear, Kenji and Suki felt justified in their actions.

Was Roni close by? Has he found her?

They heaved a sigh of relief when the ogre started moving again. They had never been in a situation like this, where they were following a creature, so far unseen by their kind, to protect their friend. But the thought that Roni could fall into the clutches of this menace terrified them both.

"Maybe we should shout out and warn her," suggested Suki with heightened anxiety.

Kenji shook his head. It was too dangerous a plan. The ogre could hear them, and that would have catastrophic results. "No, Suki. If we get caught in the hands of this…this… whatever this is…we will be in trouble with the others at Imen-Hera. Realistically, we shouldn't even be here, let alone follow Roni."

They needed to plan their move carefully to warn Roni, without being caught by the ogre and also avoid getting into trouble back home.

He looked around to see if there was a Boad tree nearby from where they could make their escape back to Imen-Hera, but there were none in sight.

The Boad trees were in greater concentration in the center of the forest and scarcer toward the outer edges. This was another safeguard built into their system to thwart the Imen from wandering out of the forest and into neighboring areas where they might be tempted by things that were disallowed.

Kenji and Suki were now close to the southern edge of the forest that butted up against the Talbot Mountain Range.

"Are you looking for a Boad tree?" she asked in a whisper.

He nodded, and they both scoured their immediate vicinity in search of one.

"I told you there're none here," she reminded him.

"You're right. I haven't seen one in a while. There are fewer trees the further you go to the outer boundaries of the forest. We might have to think this out carefully before we act," assessed Kenji.

She nodded in agreement and started glancing around, looking out for the ogre.

"Wait! What's he doing?" Suki frowned as she saw the being stop and stare in awe at whatever he was chasing.

Then suddenly, he thrashed about jubilantly as though he was possessed by a mad fervor. The creature had found something or someone.

Is it Roni?

Yes, it was! The two friends observed that his uncontrollable action had startled Roni, who turned around, and her eyes widened at the sight of the ogre. Her sudden action forced the creature to stand still.

Nobody made a movement, not even a breath, while they took in the scene in front of them. Kenji and Suki watched the creature and Roni. Roni was startled to a stop by the ogre, and said ogre also looked dumbfounded, not knowing what to do next.

Kenji and Suki watched him move his arm and struggle with the leather pouch at his hip as his thick, calloused fingers searched through it. Finally, after huffing and grunting, he pulled out something tiny from its depths, loaded it into his slingshot, and took aim.

As he was about to release the object, Suki let out a yell.

"Watch out, Roni!"

The sudden warning pierced the silence of the forest and caused the ogre to jump, and his aim was off. He fired at Roni with his slingshot, but he missed.

The tiny glass vial flew through the air and smashed against a small tree. It instantly transformed the tree into a fist-sized pebble.

Both Suki and Kenji were staggered by the witchcraft. They looked at each other in shock, and obeying a silent instinct born out of years of friendship, ran in opposite directions to confuse and distract the awkward creature, giving an opportunity for Roni to escape.

The ogre was pleased to see his sorcery skill was working well. However, he was extremely furious about missing his target and letting her vanish from his sight.

At first, he thought about investigating who yelled out, but he quickly reminded himself of the task he still needed to accomplish before Roni completely disappeared. He was so close to achieving what he wanted and was not ready to give up. He set out to chase Roni, who scrambled through the forest feverishly, keeping a watch for the white flowers marking her trail.

And hot on the ogre's heels were Suki and Kenji. They gave chase with caution, uncertain of what spell the creature might cast upon them.

Bomo trampled ahead, carrying the slingshot in his hand at the ready and keeping Roni in sight. He paused briefly to see if he had a good shot at the target, but Roni was moving too fast.

The chase took them to the edge of the forest, where the trees almost butted against the sheer cliffs of the Talbot Range.

Roni ran as fast as her legs could carry her, following the white flower trail until it abruptly terminated at a vertical mountain wall.

The Talbot Range was a smooth wall of rock extending in both directions as far as the eye could see.

Roni was completely out of breath as she paused and frantically looked back to see where her pursuer was. Although she couldn't see him approach, she could hear him clearly.

"Roni. You are mine… Wait!"

This frightened her to no end, hearing the ogre yelling out her name and declaring her as his property.

Who is he? How does he know my name? I don't remember seeing him ever. Why is he chasing me?

So many questions spun in her mind, but she didn't want to stay around to find out the answers because it was obvious he was insane and trying to harm her.

Roni looked up at the vertical rock face in front of her and wondered how to climb it. This was a difficult range to scale because the rock was sheer and high, and there was nothing to shield a person from the stark nakedness of its face. There was no place to hide. No crevices. No nooks.

She desperately searched the surface with her hands looking for the niches her father had told her about until she found them.

Hooking her fingers to one and then the other, she began climbing as fast as she could, finding the footholds that could support her further. She had ascended no more than ten feet up when her nemesis came into view.

As soon as Bomo saw her, he halted abruptly, staring at her in complete disbelief, his jaw slackened.

Roni was in plain view.

Bomo couldn't have asked for a better situation by which to trap her.

The klutz fumbled around in his pouch until he produced the second vial and loaded his slingshot.

Meanwhile, Roni was in a precarious situation where she couldn't use her zoon or any of the other weapons given to her for defense. She needed both hands to climb up the sheer wall.

As she looked down at the menacing creature, she was mortified by the wild and crazed look on his face. *What does he want from me?* she wondered. But she couldn't waste more time. She had to escape.

Moving her hands and legs faster, she pushed her body to the limits and climbed briskly to try to get away from the ogre.

Kenji and Suki followed the beast at a safe distance but soon realized they were up against the mountain range.

They saw him stop, load his slingshot once again, stretching it to its limit, and take aim at his target. There was no hesitation in his actions.

They both ran to distract him again, screaming at the top of their voices. From the corners of their eye, they saw Roni climbing up as fast as she could. However, this time, the ogre couldn't be startled, and he released the projectile smoothly, determination guiding his aim.

The vial traveled through the air and burst into shards as it struck Roni's back.

She immediately transformed into a fist-sized pebble and fell to the ground.

Both Suki and Kenji were horrified at what they had just witnessed. They remained frozen in their footsteps, not knowing what to do. They weren't sure if the ogre had killed her or what he had done to her. They just knew she was no longer there.

Suki halted in her tracks and was seized with paralyzing fear and grief at the loss of her best friend.

Kenji tried to get her attention, but she was catatonic. He shook her hard, hoping the movements would jar her awake. Luckily for him, after a few moments, she came to her senses.

"Suki, Suki! We have to do something, but I'm not sure what," Kenji stated helplessly, his tone resigned by the time he stopped speaking.

Suki remained speechless. Her entire body had grown numb, seeing the kind of wicked magic the creature could do.

Kenji gathered his courage from deep within him and decided to go closer and see what the ogre was doing and what became of their friend.

"Come on, Suki, let's see what he did to her," he suggested.

Suki shook her head in refusal. Stunned by what she had witnessed, she refused to come along. She was worried about getting into trouble when they got back home and being banished to this strange, cruel world. It was more than she could bear.

After realizing she was not going to accompany him, he asked her to hide in a safe place while he went to take a look. Suki complied and found the trunk of a large tree with a thick canopy to hide behind.

Kenji crouched low and quietly made his way toward the ogre, whom he could hear rambling something incomprehensible at a distance.

As he got closer, he could see the specimen hunched down, examining the ground carefully.

Kenji figured out that the creature had turned Roni into a pebble just like the tree, but unfortunately for Bomo, the ground was an ancient dry riverbed where water once flowed, leaving behind millions of similar river pebbles. And Roni now was one of them.

The ogre became frustrated because he couldn't identify the one that was Roni. He stomped his foot and kicked the ground and rocks, hoping the right one would perhaps let out a scream. But other than his actions kicking up dust and pebbles into the air, no scream was heard. And no Roni.

Bomo was enraged!

He turned his attention to the individuals who had tried to divert his aim. He looked in Kenji's direction, and although he couldn't see where either one of them was, he stormed in the general direction of the prior yell and screamed out loud. He would not spare anyone when he got his hands on them. He ran erratically through the forest, ranting and shouting from the top of his lungs.

Kenji was alarmed as he saw the creature charging toward him. He quickly moved to hide behind a tree as Bomo rushed past. Circling around once he could no longer see the ogre, he pulled Suki out of her hiding place, and both ran to where Roni had been last seen.

They went to the riverbed and tried to isolate the area where they thought they saw her climb and then vanish. They looked carefully to find a rock that looked different from the rest, but at first glance, they all looked alike.

Kenji could now understand why the ogre was so frustrated. He knew they had an insurmountable task in front of them if they wanted to save Roni. They began to move the rocks gently by hand to see which one it might be.

Within a few moments, they heard the menace approaching, so they quickly ran and hid again behind trees, while keeping one eye open for the ogre.

Bomo returned, mumbling curses under his breath. He resumed kicking the rocks violently in search of the "one." His leather pouch got in the way of his search. In a fit of rage, he tore it off and flung it into the bushes.

He searched the ground until he fell down in exhaustion. Then he began to move the rocks around with his slingshot and, after a while, saw one that struck him as being different.

It was a large round stone, slightly bigger than his fist, and was streaked with reddish veins. He was certain it was she. The veins were obviously her blood veins. He jumped to his feet with exuberance and irrepressible joy.

"It's 'er! I 'ave you now. You're mine. That's your veins. I 'ave you. Ha, ha, ha."

Suki was shocked.

Kenji remained calm and studied the creature, wondering if the ogre had the right rock.

The maladroit creature looked around for the leather pouch he had thrown away moments ago to put the precious item into. He found it lying next to some shrubs.

He picked it up, stuffed the rock into it, slung the bag around his neck, and disappeared. He never gave a single thought to the individuals who had tried to distract him.

Off he went. He feared no one. He had Roni. He needed no one now.

Kenji and Suki quietly emerged from their hiding places after ascertaining the wretched ogre had completely disappeared.

They went to the rocks to check for themselves, scrutinizing the ground to see if the ogre had made a mistake.

"He said something about veins, Kenji. Don't you think he'd know what he's looking for? He has our Roni," raged Suki.

She was consumed with fear, not knowing what the creature was going to do with her friend or even why he pursued her.

Kenji refused to believe the ogre had the good sense to pick out the actual stone. He too had examined the ground and moved rocks around but couldn't tell.

"I think we'd better get back before we get banished to this terrible place. I can't live here with monstrous creatures like that and not being able to use our gifts to escape," she pleaded.

Kenji felt sorry for her, and although he didn't want to return, he felt compelled to take her back. He could tell it had been a shocking experience for her, especially since they chose not to abuse their special powers.

As they began their departure, they trod carefully on the rocks just in case one of them was Roni.

Suki noticed a rock by her foot marbled with red veins.

"Look!" she exclaimed, pointing to it. "That one has veins also. Could it be he has a similar stone? The wrong stone?" She crouched down to pick it up.

They both examined it carefully, and it seemed to fit the description of what the ogre had departed with.

Kenji became hopeful the ogre had taken just an ordinary stone and that Roni was still somewhere in this cascade of rocks.

He leaped from one stone to the next, looking at all of them in his vicinity. After checking around, he found another one at a distance.

Kenji and Suki covered a large area in their search and found at least five similar stones.

They concluded the ogre might have taken just an ordinary rock, meaning Roni could still be somewhere in the pile.

"Is she alive?" Suki verbalized her biggest fear in a quivering voice.

"But why would he kill her? Didn't he just pick up a rock thinking it to be her?"

"True. He's a sorcerer, Kenji, and that means he has the ability to change her back," she reasoned.

Kenji was not completely convinced the hideous creature possessed the mental faculties to be an actual sorcerer. "A sorcerer? He seemed too unintelligent for that."

"He had enough intelligence to turn her to stone, didn't he?" she rebutted. "Let's not underestimate him."

Both agreed being cautious would be more prudent at this point.

They noticed that shadows were drawn across the landscape, concluding the day. Soon it would be dusk, shortly followed by nightfall.

They wanted to remain there and search the piles of rocks to find her, but they knew time was not on their side. After much debate, they decided to return home before nightfall and come back the next morning to resume their search.

"Kenji! What if he realizes the rock is not her and decides to come back in the morning and look for her as well?" asked Suki in a state of panic.

"Don't worry, we'll be here at dawn. And if he shows up…well, if he shows up, then…I'll do whatever it takes to keep him away," he replied, having made the resolve he would take the chance to use his powers for this noble act and if he were banished for it, then so be it.

Suki gathered he had made this decision after a lot of thought and became very anxious. She didn't want to be banished or live there. She loved Imen-Hera, and that is where she belonged.

Kenji knew she would be strongly against the idea, so he took the time to explain it to her.

"I understand your apprehension, and you don't have to come with me. I've made up my mind to come out here tomorrow and do whatever it takes to find her. I'm willing to live with the consequences. I have to help Roni," he stated in a gentle but firm tone.

Suki didn't reply to this and quietly pondered what he said. She admired his sense of duty and self-sacrifice in doing the right thing. She was torn between wanting to go with him and desiring to continue her simple life. She was in a dilemma. She couldn't change Kenji's mind, nor did she want to take a chance with her future.

She liked the predictability and wasn't too keen on a life filled with random situations that she had little control over.

They walked at a faster pace as the shadows grew long and finally reached a Boad tree and returned home to safety.

Kenji wondered if Suki would come with him the next morning, but she said nothing and walked to her quarters quietly.

KING AUDUN STORMED OFF to tend to his guests. He had the responsibility of breaking the news about Eyvind to Camden, Tara, and Adina but didn't anticipate much resistance, especially since Adina was supposedly in love with Korin.

Meanwhile, Aurelius and his soldiers escorted Eyvind, Raidon, and Axel through the town en route to the forest. Aurelius had yearned for this day all his life. He despised Eyvind, for he embodied everything Aurelius was not, and detested all those who pledged their loyalties to the young Prince. This was indeed the opportunity of a lifetime.

Eyvind and the Knights had their hands bound and their bodies draped in ordinary hooded cloaks pulled low over their faces to conceal their identities. They had lost their rights to the royal regalia with the insignia of the Imperial Knights. The last thing this Kingdom needed was civil unrest, and if the public caught sight of their beloved Eyvind as a prisoner, it would lead to chaos of unimaginable proportions.

The three prisoners were led out of the city and down the path toward the forest. Upon reaching the edge of the woods, their cloaks were removed, and Aurelius ordered them to lead the way to the cave where the woodcutter was last seen.

The friends looked at one another and used gestures and facial expressions to devise an escape plan. Aurelius was well aware of their capabilities and knew they would flee, especially since they had the upper hand of knowing the forest better than most.

Aurelius signaled his men, and the soldiers closed in on Eyvind and the Knights and monitored their every move, riding behind them at all times with their hands firmly planted on the hilts of their swords.

Eight well-built soldiers, three prisoners, and a Royal Minister trekked through the forest, with Raidon taking the lead. Aurelius kept the party of men in a single file to avoid contact between them. He didn't want to take any chances and knew he had to be alert the entire way. They rode deep into the belly of the forest and then off the trail until they arrived at the cave where Laris had been found slain.

Aurelius dismounted his horse and demanded a torch, which was immediately handed to him by one of the soldiers. He went into the dark cavern to examine what lay within.

There was freshly hewn rubble scattered on the ground. He picked up a few pieces and held them up to the torch to examine them closely. Most of it was just bits of rock.

However, he found a piece with tiny specks of gold. His eyes lit up, and he wanted to find the woodcutter at all costs. At this point, he realized that the vial had already been used for the transformation based on the specks of gold.

Aurelius was furious! However, he wanted to locate the woodcutter in case he still had some drops left.

He emerged from the cave and confronted Axel and Raidon.

"You imbeciles! He's already used the entire potion or at least some of it. Did you not gather that from all this hewn rock, speckled with gold?" His shrill voice echoed through the forest, and in return, both men maintained their silence and refused to comment.

"He may still have the vial in his possession," stated Eyvind.

Aurelius gave them all a look of sheer disgust and instructed them to dismount the horses to begin their task of tracking the woodcutter as well as the Imen woman.

"Don't think of fooling me anymore. It would take me not more than a few seconds to drive this sword into your treacherous hearts. You hear me? Now get to working. Find me the woodcutter and the woman and no tricks from any of you!"

Aurelius kept each man as separate from the other as possible. This made it difficult for the three to devise an escape plan.

They searched the ground for clues and found large undisturbed footprints. They followed them through the brush to a clearing where they saw hoof and cartwheel tracks.

Raidon, Axel, and Eyvind knew their fate—they were not going to leave the forest alive. Aurelius had already made several remarks insinuating their outcome. They had to find a way to get away. They had one shot at it, and they had to be ready to take it.

The trio followed the tracks through the forest.

Aurelius and the rest of the soldiers remained on their horses in close proximity to Eyvind and his men.

Little did Aurelius know that the Knights had enough training to communicate with one another without drawing suspicion from the soldiers despite their close watchful eyes.

They reached an area with several oxcart tracks marked on the ground and deliberately followed the one leading to the outskirts of the forest. They went around in several confusing circles to disorient the soldiers and then followed the trail that Bomo left some time ago on one of his treks to the city to sell wood.

The day wore away, and Aurelius became very frustrated with each passing hour. He made several threats to their lives if they came up empty. "You better listen and listen hard, the three of you. If you try to fool me, you'll be introduced to a side of me that you have not yet seen. Understood?" His words were deep and imposing, and his tone laced with authority.

The superior intonation grated on Axel's nerves, and he itched to get his hands on him. He wanted to charge at Aurelius' horse and knock him to the ground and break his neck. However, he resisted the temptation and waited for Eyvind's cue for the next move.

Eyvind ignored Aurelius' threats and continued tracking in the wrong direction, knowing attacking the minister would have their deaths looming faster over them. The soldiers would not allow such an act to go unpunished.

The day came to a conclusion, and night befell upon them. They were still following the trail with no end in sight.

"What sort of trackers are you? A blind man could have found the woodcutter by now and as far as I can tell..." Aurelius then paused and looked around. "Wait a minute! We've been going in a circle...if I'm not mistaken." His scream of fury reverberated across the forest, making even the night animals go silent.

Aurelius grabbed Eyvind by his collar, his entire demeanor threatening to do him bodily harm if he did not track down the woodcutter's lair or the woman.

"I've had enough of this. You better lead me to the woodcutter before I shove this sword through your torso and leave you here to die. You understand?" he shrieked and kicked Eyvind in the chest, knocking him down. "I'll give you one final chance to find this woodcutter and the Imen woman, and if you fail me, I'll carve you all like meat with my blade." Aurelius bent down and grazed the tip of his shiny sword across Eyvind's face.

Axel stood by, watching Aurelius exercise his ruthless tactics on the young Prince, but he had reached a point where he was unwilling to tolerate it any further. Axel could no longer be an idle bystander.

He charged at Aurelius.

However, the soldiers grabbed him quickly and stopped him dead in his tracks.

"I wouldn't try that if I were you. You're in no position to show valor," Aurelius stated as he turned and drove his blade right into Axel's chest, leaving everyone shocked, including his own soldiers.

Raidon and Eyvind were horrified by what they just witnessed. It was a rash display of power.

Axel gasped for breath, his hands clutching the wound. Blood seeped out from between his fingers, his life slipping away fast. The sword had found its mark. Soon his lifeless body slumped forward and fell into a heap.

"Let this be a lesson to both of you. I won't tolerate further mockery of being toted around this wretched forest and made a fool of. You will lead me to the woodcutter and that woman first thing in the morning," he barked out, stepping over Axel's body, indifferent to a life lost.

Eyvind and Raidon were enraged and shocked at Aurelius' irrational actions. They tried to get to him but were held down by the soldiers and overpowered.

Aurelius walked away, refusing to give them any further audience.

The subdued prisoners yelled out curses that echoed through the forest like the roar of a beast beckoning to be unleashed. They struggled with the soldiers for a while, but in the end, they too fell to their knees in deep sorrow.

Axel remained where he fell until a soldier yanked the blade from his chest and draped a cloak over him. He wiped the blood off the sword, using the edge of the cloak, and gave it to Aurelius, who returned it to his sheath without compunction.

Raidon and Eyvind couldn't bear to look at Aurelius or their fallen brethren. They were grief-struck. Speech was beyond them as each contemplated what they should do next.

The other soldiers began to set up camp as nightfall was running close to the heels of dusk.

Aurelius instructed two soldiers to dig a ditch and inter the body before it got dark.

The people of Carron and surrounding regions cremated their dead to release the souls into the afterlife. Interring the dead was the worst possible act because it was believed that it trapped the soul and prevented its release.

Eyvind and Raidon couldn't bear to watch this done to Axel.

"Let him suffer in his interred prison forever," Aurelius remarked, his laughter mocking them.

Eyvind wanted to charge and strike him, but Raidon motioned him to stop.

"You'll soon join your brethren if you don't give me what I want," Aurelius added with barbed cynicism.

Eyvind and Raidon found it difficult to sleep that night. They were awake for hours tormented by Axel's death until exhaustion overcame them, and they finally slipped into a restless slumber.

In the morning, they were jarred from their sleep by sharp kicks to the ribs delivered by Aurelius.

"Wake up, my beauties. We're not here on leisure. You have a task at hand. Now, get up!" he roared as he delivered another kick to both of them.

Raidon and Eyvind were startled by this rude awakening, which knocked the wind out of them, and gasped for breath as they stumbled to their feet.

Aurelius and his soldiers mounted their horses and pushed the two prisoners forward to lead the way on foot.

Eyvind hesitated and looked one last time in the direction of the mound beneath which Axel's body lay buried.

"Take a good look. You'll soon join him. I promise I won't keep you apart too long," Aurelius mocked, laughing wickedly.

Raidon was furious but felt helpless. They had to figure out a way to escape, no matter what. They just needed enough time to remove Axel from the suffocating grave and release his soul through cremation. It had to be done even if it meant risking their own lives.

But first, they had another task in front of them. Today was their day of reckoning. They began their trek back deep into the belly of the forest to search for the woodcutter and the Imen. Raidon and Eyvind were determined to escape and had to plan carefully. However, they were being closely monitored. Being outnumbered, the eight burly soldiers could easily overpower them. Also, Aurelius was alert to their sudden movements.

Every so often, Aurelius struck them with his horsewhip as a reminder to follow the actual tracks and not pull a fast one as they had done the previous day.

It wasn't long before they heard a loud cry echo through the forest, which sounded like a wounded beast. They halted at once to figure out what it was.

The monstrous roar unnerved Aurelius the most. He disliked the forest and all the creatures that dwelt within it. Upon hearing the ominous cry, he felt justified for never wanting to journey into this territory.

"What was that?" he asked in alarm.

The soldiers looked around to see where the sound emanated from, but it was too hard to tell because it seemed to come from all around. They drew their blades out and got into their formation, prepared to take on the beast.

Raidon and Eyvind had never heard such a roar either, and they too had no clue what it was. Yet, they remained calm and alert because they were used to dangerous animals.

Aurelius noticed the menacing roar had no effect on his prisoners and immediately suspected he was being led to a trap.

Unbeknownst to any of them, those were the groans of the insane woodcutter echoing through the forest.

"Is this part of your plan? To have us ambushed by some wild creature?" he asked in a fit of rage as he kicked and punched Eyvind, who fell to the ground with blood streaming from his mouth.

"Aurelius! We don't know what that is either, and we're not planning an ambush," pleaded Raidon on Eyvind's behalf, who now sat crumpled on the ground.

"Silence! You both take me for a fool, don't you? We'll see about that," he warned as he kicked Raidon in the chest, drew his blade out once again, and approached Eyvind.

I T WAS EARLY MORNING, and Kenji was just getting up to begin his lone trek back to the edge of the forest to search for Roni from amongst the million other rocks.

He wondered if Suki was going to change her mind and come along, but it seemed she wouldn't.

He got dressed and prepared to leave when the forest siren rang through Imen-Hera. Instinctively he harmonized with it—a force of habit from hanging out with Roni.

After he did so, he realized he was now bound to attend, and that would cut into the time he had to find Roni before the ogre arrived.

He was stuck in a quandary and uncertain about what to do. As he wrestled with his dilemma, Suki appeared and looked worried as always.

"Did you answer the siren?" she asked fearfully. She hoped he hadn't because she was still startled by the events of the previous day.

He was surprised to see her. "Yes, I did," he replied in dismay.

"Are you still going up there? To the edge of the forest?" she asked timidly.

"Yes, I was. I mean, yes, I am, but I accepted the call for help, and now I'm bound by it." Worry coated his words.

"It is your duty first and foremost, Kenji," she reminded him gently. Although she loved Roni dearly, Suki felt it was their responsibility as Imen to tend to the tasks bestowed upon them and not deviate.

"I know my obligations, and I haven't forgotten," he answered with a hint of annoyance.

Suki could see the distress in Kenji's eyes, and fighting with her inner instinct to stay safe, she threw caution to the wind and decided to help expedite the call so Kenji could go on his way to execute what he had set out to do in the first place.

"I'll come with you, Kenji," she declared.

Kenji was shocked but didn't refuse the company. He loved the support she was giving him, and smiling, they set off to find the source of the alarm.

As they emerged in the forest, they heard yelling at a fairly short distance, that echoed around them. They made their way toward it and got to the source of the commotion.

At a distance, they saw several soldiers standing around armed, and on the ground were two men with their heads bowed, who appeared to be hurt, with another man in imperial clothes standing over them in a threatening manner, with his blade drawn, about to drive it through one of them.

They rushed toward them as fast as they could and slowed time until everyone seemed to be frozen. They could see the blade just inches away from the injured man on the ground.

Suki and Kenji hurried over and stood beside Aurelius.

Kenji pushed Aurelius' blade aside gently and sat down to examine the injured man.

Suki was startled when she realized the two men were the hunters they had helped in the recent past. The injured man was the one over whom Roni was banished.

"It's him!" she shrieked, pointing to the man.

Kenji pulled back and lifted his eyes to the injured man's face and noticed it was indeed the hunter. Eyvind.

He looked at the other man sitting on the ground beside him, and he too looked familiar. He was one of the three who had accompanied him that day.

"It is them!" he agreed. Kenji couldn't believe his luck.

He had a brilliant idea. He quickly dragged Eyvind away as far as he could and instructed Suki to tend to his injuries while he went back to get the other.

After dragging them both to safety, Kenji resumed time to its normal pace.

Eyvind and Raidon were shocked to find themselves elsewhere. Just seconds prior, they both were facing certain death, and the next moment, they had been carted away from the threat and rescued. They couldn't understand what had just occurred.

Suki and Kenji motioned them to remain silent and follow them. They took both men to a denser and safer area of the forest where they tended to their injuries.

"You look familiar. Where are we?" asked Raidon, looking at his rescuers. "Now I remember. You were there the day Sire was injured by the boar."

"Yes, we were," answered Kenji.

Eyvind looked around for Roni and wondered where she was. "Where's Roni?"

Kenji and Suki were astounded he knew her name.

"How'd you know her name?" asked Suki in surprise.

"She told me," he answered.

"Told you? When?" questioned Kenji in shock. He didn't remember meeting them any other time. "You've met Roni more than one time?"

"Yes, I have. The two of you weren't there, but she rescued a deer I was hunting," he explained. He couldn't figure out why this was of such concern to them. However, he politely answered their questions.

"Alone? To save a deer?" asked Kenji. It made no sense to him.

"Yes. Is something wrong?" asked Eyvind, sensing uneasiness in Kenji's voice and demeanor.

Kenji realized he was prying into something that was irrelevant at that moment.

"Who were those men?" he asked, changing the subject.

"That was Aurelius, the minister of all the prefectures within Carron, and his loyal thugs," replied Raidon with disdain. None of it made any sense to them, and Eyvind recognized that.

"Let's just say he's an important person where we come from, and he's carrying out his wicked duties," Eyvind simplified.

Kenji and Suki both nodded in confusion. They were unable to relate to this since their world was devoid of such ugliness. They knew Eyvind was also a person of importance because the others referred to him as Sire.

"And who're you? You're important as well, right?" asked Kenji.

Eyvind's mind regressed to the conversation he had with his father the previous day when he'd surrendered his title. He was a prince then, but now he was just an ordinary citizen.

"I'm Eyvind, and until yesterday morning, I *was* a person of importance, but now I'm a fugitive," he replied without much concern.

Kenji wanted to know everything. However, he knew this was not the right time to question him about the circumstances that led to his present state. They had pressing matters at hand.

"How well do you know Roni?" asked Kenji.

"It's strange, but I feel like I've known her all my life even though I've only met her twice. Where is she, by the way?" he asked, looking around for her enthusiastically.

Kenji chose not to answer the question at this time. They needed to find a safer place and then discuss the other matters.

"We must leave. Your men will find us soon if we don't go right away," replied Kenji as he directed them to the path that would lead them to safety.

They crouched down low and made their way through the forest until they were at a safe distance from Aurelius and his men.

Suki wondered what Kenji had up his sleeve.

They hid behind a large rock that was surrounded by thick vegetation. They were well concealed.

Suki looked frightened and wanted to leave and go back. As far as she was concerned, she had performed her duty, and the rest was up to these men.

Kenji had a different plan, however. He wondered if Eyvind would be able to distinguish Roni from all the other rocks that were scattered in the riverbed and help him find her.

He went on to tell them what happened to Roni as both men stood astounded.

"It's that woodcutter, Eyvind! I knew he was up to no good that day. I should have apprehended him when I had the chance," exclaimed Raidon.

"Take me there at once," pleaded Eyvind. "I just hope the woodcutter hasn't found her first. Where did he learn such sorcery?"

No one offered an answer because they too didn't know.

Kenji looked at Suki, who was torn between going with them and returning to Imen-Hera. She feared breaking any law that would land her in the same situation as Roni. Kenji could see the struggle and indecision that Suki faced and made it easy for her.

"I think you better return home," he suggested. She hesitated for a moment and then turned to leave.

Kenji felt awkward being left alone initially since he had never been in the forest by himself for any reason. Then his reasoning and determination took over.

Raidon and Eyvind thanked Suki for helping them and left with Kenji.

As they were departing, Suki called out to them, "Wait!"

Kenji was alarmed and came running back to see what she wanted. "What's the matter?"

She remained silent and grabbed him by his arm and led him towards Raidon and Eyvind.

"Let's go!" she ordered. Kenji was puzzled.

"I thought…well, never mind." He didn't want to question her about her change of mind. He was just glad she was willing to come along.

The party set off in the direction of the Talbot Mountains, where Roni had been last seen.

AURELIUS SHRIEKED LOUDLY, "WHERE did they go? What kind of sorcery was that? I knew they couldn't be trusted. I knew they were up to something." He sliced the air with his blade as he questioned the soldiers about Eyvind's and Raidon's whereabouts.

His soldiers were just as dumbfounded as he, but as always, Aurelius suspected them. He questioned their loyalties and convinced himself they might have been secretly loyal to Eyvind and aided in his escape.

Aurelius continued to intimidate and threaten his men to make sure they weren't lying or involved in the escape. Frustrated and in anger, in the end, he felt he had no other choice but to send a couple of them to look for the escaped prisoners.

He was astonished by the sophistication of the sorcery—if only he could get his hands on the witchcraft that had aided their escape. He wondered what magic had caused them to vanish into thin air right before his eyes.

Aurelius paced the floor of the forest, agonizing over this mystery, and became even more obsessed, craving it for himself more than ever. He changed his mind and mounted his horse to personally search for the prisoners because he didn't trust his men despite their assertions of having no knowledge of the whereabouts of the escapees.

He viciously struck his horse with his whip and aimlessly steered him from side to side, avoiding the dense thicket of trees that came at him one after the other. There was nothing systematic about his search. And soon he had to admit defeat. He had no idea what he was doing, as he had never gone on a search before. And going this way and that would only get him lost and unable to find his way back. Worse, the two escapees might ambush him, seeing he was alone. He panicked at the thought.

He realized he was now on their turf and at a disadvantage. The minister stopped abruptly and looked around to see if he could catch a glimpse of either of them and then began his way back. He craned his neck to the left and right to listen for the sounds of disturbance, but the forest remained quiet, and the only disruptive sounds were those he was making while tearing through the woods, trying to find his way to his men. He sent out the rest of his soldiers in different directions to search for Eyvind and Raidon.

The crazed minister waited for the search parties to return, pacing the floor of the forest.

Eventually, they returned one by one but without the prisoners, fearing his wrath at coming back empty-handed.

Then one of them spoke up. "Sire, I can probably track the woodcutter. I have done it before."

Aurelius was not impressed, but at this point, he had no other alternatives.

The soldier marched ahead, and the rest followed in a single file behind him.

THE OGRE REACHED HIS habitat and looked around for any signs of soldiers who might want to ambush him. It was late in the evening, and long shadows were cast on the ground. Bomo was having a hard time seeing anything in the darkness. He waited a moment or two to hear the slightest whisper that would warn him of intruders, but silence surrounded him. It was safe to approach his front door. He ran as fast as he could and unlocked it with his big, worn key.

Stepping inside, he slammed the door shut behind him and quickly bolted it. He didn't want to be disturbed. Barricading room after room with furniture, he reached his study and collapsed on a rickety chair. He paused to take a huge, noisy breath and set out to work.

He leaned forward and pulled out the ancient Book of Spells, opened it to the Callioux spell, and began to read how to reverse it. He nodded his gigantic head and patted the rock in the leather pouch at his hip. His golden-yellow eyes began to glitter with a crazed fervor, malice radiating through them. It was a frightening sight to behold.

He began to assemble all the necessary ingredients for the spell until he realized it called for a live lizard heart.

"Dat's easy. Dere's always lizards in the woodpile," he told the lone cell in his brain aloud, filled with confidence.

Bomo rushed to take down the barricades one after the other until he burst outside. By the time he opened the front door and stepped out, he noticed it was now completely pitch dark.

He went back inside and returned with a torch. The ogre shoved the lit torch into the dark recesses of the woodpile and peered in. "'Ere lizards, come 'ere, little lizards," he beckoned them like an overgrown child.

He inspected the massive pile of wood back to front and side to side, searching the cracks, but no lizard was in sight. With each round of search, his anger kept rising.

"Why can't I find a lizard when I need one? All day long, this woodpile has lizards crawling over it. Now, nothin'."

He became so enraged that he kicked and toppled the pile of wood. Grunting and moaning, he threw pieces of wood in all directions, until he had leveled the entire pile. He picked up his torch and searched the entire area of scattered wood to find the single lizard that he needed. No. None. He couldn't believe his rotten luck.

Eventually, he gave up and went back in, as usual bolting and barricading each room he passed by. On his bed, he grabbed the smooth pebble from the leather pouch and held it close to his bosom as his eyes drifted closed. He tried to stay awake, but sleep overcame him, and soon his snores were the only sounds vibrating in the room.

He woke up at daybreak and rushed out to look for a lizard. He was met with the chaos of the logs scattered across the ground, the action of his anger from the night before. He berated himself for the mess he had created. But seeing that he had more urgent business at hand, he set off in search of his lizard, grinning maniacally at one thought.

"I 'ave Roni. I'll get all the gold in the world. I don't need to chop wood 'ver again."

He lamely tried to balance himself on pieces of wood and fell multiple times because he lacked the right coordination to control his awkward physique. He saw something slithering across the log and pounced on it as it tried to escape. But desperation came with its own dexterity, and Bomo had that lizard in his grasp. He rushed back into the house and quickly barricaded the doors with extra care this time.

He was taking no chances.

In his study, he poured over the list to verify each ingredient again and again until he was satisfied. Keeping all the necessary items in front of him, he set to work.

Bomo built a fire and placed a gigantic cauldron upon it. Slowly, he added each item as per the instructions.

He hovered over the dark cauldron, eager and gleeful, like an expectant father, stirring it ever so slowly while mumbling all kinds of strange things under his breath.

Eventually, the potion was done, and the specimen rose to his feet in elation.

"Mine! All mine! No one can ever 'arm me anymore," he declared to the world.

Then he reached into the pouch and produced the pebble with the reddish marbling.

"Roni... Roni... Roni... Soon, very soon, m'dear. You'll be all mine," he muttered as tears of elation welled in his eyes.

Bomo carried on talking to the rock as he held it up to his big ugly mouth and kissed it with his fleshy, protruding lips. He placed it in a dented metal tub, spooned out the disgusting crude from the cauldron with a big ladle, and gently poured it over the rock.

At first, he squinted his eyes shut, not knowing what to expect.

However, he couldn't stand the suspense and immediately opened them. Shock zapped through him. He stared down at the rock smothered with the muck, but no transformation had taken place. It remained unchanged. He couldn't believe his eyes. He waited for a few more minutes to see if it needed time to soak through, but nothing changed.

His eyes began to glow with rage as he dished out another ladleful from the cauldron, poured it over the rock, and waited some more.

Still, not a thing changed. Wrath poured out from him as he kept adding spoonfuls of the crude into the tub, but the rock remained unchanged.

In complete fury, the clumsy clod hit the rock with the ladle in full swing. The rock clanged against the metal tub but still remained unchanged. He picked up the cauldron in a frenzy and poured the entire content into the tub, hoping for some result.

Again, nothing occurred.

The ogre went wild.

He picked up furniture and threw it against the walls and shattered anything in his path. He shoved the barricades, stamped on them, and broke a few until he reached outside, where he let out a wild, roaring cry that thundered through the forest.

He ran around in a fit of rage, smashing and kicking anything in his path.

Once he was done and his rage abated to some extent, he went back in, hoping by some miracle, the rock had now transformed.

He slowly walked into his study, hoping to see Roni standing there in the tub, but to his dismay, the metal tub remained on the floor with the rock submerged in the crude just as he had left it.

He couldn't believe it.

He grabbed the Book of Spells and scrutinized each word, wondering what had gone wrong.

He recalled every ingredient and the order they were to be cast into the pot. He had done everything correctly.

"Then why won't it work?" he cried out.

He smashed the book against his head.

When he was done with his fit, a thought pierced the lone cell in his brain.

'Ave I picked up the right rock?

The very thought of having picked the wrong one struck him like lightning.

'Ow could it be? There wozn't another rock like it around. Besides, this one has 'er blood veins.

He reasoned with his brain, trying to come up with something. He picked up the ladle and fished the rock out of the mucky contents of the tub and examined it.

Are dey veins? He stared at it closely, second-guessing his observations.

The ogre picked up a large knife and brutally tried to slice the rock across one of the veins. He was expecting blood to pour forth; however, no such miracle occurred.

He couldn't come to grips with the fact that he had perhaps picked up the wrong rock. Bomo couldn't explain the failure of the transformation in any way other than the fact the *callioux* in his hand was just an ordinary rock and not Roni.

The enraged beast tried to crush the rock with his bare hands, squeezing his fingers tight. His face contorted as noisy grunts poured out from his large, gaping mouth.

He took the rock and flung it against the wall, where it ricocheted and smashed against the floor but stayed intact. In a fit of rage, he ran outside and threw it deep into the forest.

Bomo eventually calmed down and walked back to his lair to prepare to return to the spot where he had transformed Roni into a *callioux*.

This time he was going to find her.

THE SMALL PARTY OF four walked forth in a hurry. Kenji was in the lead with Suki close at his heels, followed by Eyvind and Raidon in the rear.

Eyvind wished he had his horse, especially at a time like this. They had to reach the mountain range before the woodcutter, just in case the ogre figured out he had the wrong stone.

Quickly, they cut their way through the trees until they saw the Talbot Mountain Range at a distance. They were hopeful but at the same time were not certain if the woodcutter had beaten them there.

They halted when the dry riverbed came into view and checked around to see if the coast was clear of the ogre and then approached with extreme caution to the place where Suki and Kenji last saw Roni.

All four trod carefully and examined each and every rock in their vicinity. Most looked alike. It was difficult to tell one from the other. Any one of them could have been Roni.

The gray landscape of pebbles played tricks on their eyes. They began to see things that were not there. Some rocks looked very different from a distance, but upon closer examination turned out to be ordinary.

Then Suki yelled out, "Look! Over there." She pointed to an object that glistened in the sunlight.

They rushed to see what it was and saw a small glass vial.

Eyvind picked it up and looked at it closely. It had a thin leather cord attached to the stopper.

Kenji and Suki moved in closer to have a better look and noticed it belonged to Kimiko, who wore it around her neck.

"That belongs to Empress Kimiko!" exclaimed Suki.

"Yes, it does. She must have given it to Roni before she left," Kenji agreed.

"Empress?" asked Eyvind.

"Yes. Kimiko is Roni's mother," Suki explained.

"Roni is a Princess?" he asked. He was astounded.

"Yes, she is," replied Kenji as he handed the vial to Eyvind. "This belongs to her. You can return it to her."

Eyvind took it from him and put it around his neck.

"Let's look over here. She was roughly in this area. Wasn't she?" Suki recalled, pointing to the area surrounding the spot where the vial was found.

They got busy looking around at every single rock one by one. They were careful yet fast. They had to find Roni before the bumbling ogre or even Aurelius and his men found them. Raidon kept watch as the three started scanning the rocks.

Then all of a sudden, Raidon rushed over to warn them about the approaching thunder of hooves. He could tell by the resonance there were several riders, which led him to believe it could only be Aurelius.

They quickened their pace and searched feverishly.

Suki was petrified, her hands trembling with fright. She wished she were back home in Imen-Hera and regretted coming along.

"I could slow down time so that we can look a little longer," suggested Kenji.

Suki was mortified by his suggestion and gave him a scolding glare.

"I would never forgive myself for allowing you to use your powers for unintended purposes. Look at what happened to Roni. I couldn't bear to see you join her in this place," replied Eyvind.

Suki let out a sigh of relief.

"Eyvind! They're getting closer," alerted Raidon in an urgent tone.

Eyvind asked Kenji and Suki to leave while he continued to comb the area. They could now hear the thundering gallop of approaching horses. They were close.

"Sire!" Raidon pleaded with even greater urgency.

Eyvind scanned the ground one last time before departing, but he wasn't having much luck.

By now, they heard voices as well as the galloping hooves.

Aurelius and his men were almost out of the forest and up against the mountain range.

Eyvind ducked low before departing and noticed a rock lying at the edge that caught his attention. It looked the same as the others.

However, it had a strange trait that didn't seem to be present in the rest. He snatched it from the ground and rushed to join the others in hiding.

Raidon noticed the rock in Eyvind's hands.

"What's that? Is it the one?" he inquired in a whisper.

His question prompted Kenji and Suki to both turn around and see what Eyvind had found.

"Do you have it?" asked Kenji in excitement.

Eyvind could not say for sure until he examined it more closely. "Let's hope it is," he replied.

They continued to push deeper into the shadows to ascertain their safety and keep as far away from Aurelius and his men as they could.

By now, the soldiers were at the foot of the mountain.

They wondered how Aurelius had tracked them.

"They couldn't possibly have tracked us here," observed Raidon. "None of them are trackers, and also they came from a different direction than us."

"That's right!" replied Eyvind.

They stopped to see if they could hear anything before making their way deeper into the forest. At first, it was hard to make out the conversation because the distance was too great.

However, it wasn't long before they heard Aurelius bark out loud, "You better look hard and find it if you want to live!"

"It's the woodcutter. They found him!" replied Raidon in astonishment.

Eyvind was less interested in the woodcutter and more in the rock he held in his hand. He lifted it to his eye level and examined it carefully. At first, it looked ordinary.

"Looks just like any other to me," commented Raidon.

Kenji and Suki nodded in agreement.

Eyvind pointed to a thin quartz vein that ran through the opaque gray stone, and by rotating it in the sunlight and carefully examining it, he could see something bluish embedded deep within. It was a bluish stone.

"Looks like a blue stone in there. Doesn't it?" pointed out Eyvind.

"Yes, I see it," exclaimed Suki, excitement building in her tone. "It looks like the one in her ring."

It was probable but unconfirmed.

Raidon walked back a few feet to check what Aurelius and his men were up to, but the distance was too much for him to see anything. "I think we better leave," he recommended.

Eyvind put the stone in his pocket, and they ran as fast as they could while maintaining their stealth until they were at a safe distance. They slowed down once they reached an area of dense vegetation and began to walk into the depths of it, all the while thinking about how they were going to get Roni back or if at all.

Eyvind carefully pulled out the rock from his pocket.

Suki took the rock from him and held it gently in her hands and reassured it, "Our sweet Roni, I promise we'll try to bring you back. You won't be trapped in there for long."

She looked to Eyvind and Raidon for assurance that they would indeed help release her friend from this ghastly form.

Both Raidon and Eyvind had no idea how they were going to accomplish this task, but they nodded and vowed not to rest until Roni was returned to her natural state. Their words comforted Suki and put to rest her heightened anxiety.

Kenji remained silent for the most part, as he normally kept his emotions to himself. He felt responsible for the state Roni was in. If only he had yelled out to distract the ogre a moment earlier, she might have been spared.

Suki noticed Kenji's silence and stepped away to offer words of comfort to him. She could feel the waves of guilt emanating from him.

Meanwhile, Eyvind and Raidon formulated a plan of how they were going to help reverse the spell. They thought hard until they arrived at a conclusion.

They needed the creature to divulge the spell that would transform Roni back to her previous state or find the spell he had used. They were excited to get going but were aware they didn't have much time because there was no doubt Aurelius would return with or without the ogre to seek the spell that was in Bomo's possession.

Eyvind approached Suki and Kenji, informed them of his plans, and requested them to return to Imen-Hera for their safety.

At first, Kenji refused and insisted on coming along with them, but after Eyvind explained to him about Aurelius' lust for sorcery and how they might fall prisoners to him, he became convinced to leave with Suki. They faded away the next second, rushing through the forest toward its center in the direction of a Boad tree.

Meanwhile, Eyvind and Raidon continued to follow the horse tracks. They could easily trace them back to the place where Aurelius had found the ogre. Hopefully, it led them to the ogre's home.

"Sire? Did you notice Suki and Kenji are no longer with us? We didn't hear their receding footsteps," Raidon commented with a smile.

"Yes. Strange, isn't it?" replied Eyvind.

These gentle creatures no longer mystified them because they understood their world and respected them more than ever.

"There it is." Raidon pointed to the trail the horses had blazed.

They ran in its direction and followed it until they reached the point where the woodcutter had been accosted.

It wasn't hard to trace the clumsy ogre. He had footprints that were so unusual that even a complete idiot could track him back.

The heavy footsteps led them to his lair, where they found piles of wood scattered all around. They could not figure out what had happened there.

It was a strange dwelling, a tiny cottage abutting a hillock, and upon closer inspection, they could see that it extended deep into the hillside.

Eyvind made his way up to the door and put his ear against it to listen for anything stirring inside. He couldn't hear a thing. He waited for a moment or two, but nothing moved.

Meanwhile, Raidon walked around the property and tried to look through the two small windows found on the entire structure. He couldn't see anything because thick burlap pieces were tacked to the windows on the inside to keep out the prying eyes.

Raidon circled back and met up with Eyvind by the front door. They tried to open it, but it was bolted shut.

Both men muscled it open. It took several attempts before it gave way.

They walked in and saw the chaotic environment in which the specimen lived. It quickly became apparent that no one else lived with him. However, they still couldn't be too sure.

The air felt heavy and damp, and musty smells surrounded them, making it difficult for them to breathe.

Eyvind and Raidon wondered what the woodcutter could want from Roni. But whatever it was, it couldn't be something honest. They looked at each other as a thought struck them.

"Sire, do you think he knows who Roni is and what gifts she possesses?"

"I think so, Raidon, seeing that he transformed her into a stone to carry her in a pouch."

They were both apprehensive about proceeding into the cottage with its broken furniture and strewn items. It could be a death trap for all they knew. Several ambushes and snares could lay hidden under the clutter unbeknownst to them. They put their trepidations behind them and quickly moved through the room, placing their feet carefully.

"Let's begin," encouraged Eyvind.

"Begin where? It's a complete pigsty. How can anyone live like this? Who knows what lurks beneath this jumble?" Raidon commented with disgust as he made his way deeper into the house. "What're we looking for, Eyvind?"

"Spells. Any book with spells?" he replied.

They both walked from one room to the next. Piles of furniture were thrown about, and the clutter continued from room to room until they reached the secret study.

After establishing there was no one else in the dwelling, Raidon returned to the front door to keep a lookout in case anyone returned.

Inside the study, Eyvind looked around and saw the cauldron lying on its side with broken bric-a-brac thrown about all over the room.

A metal tub sat on the floor with a strange dark and murky concoction in it. There were books scattered all over with their spines broken, and most were on sorcery and spells. Which one could it be?

Eyvind sifted through several volumes one after the other in a frenzy to find the spell, but there were far too many, and he soon became overwhelmed.

However, something eventually caught his sight—a big book sitting open in a corner on the desk. It was the only one that had no damage done to it.

He stumbled over the clutter to reach for it and found that it was an ancient Book of Spells... that had been opened to the Callioux spell.

Eyvind was astonished by his luck. He grabbed it and began to pour over it.

He wondered if the contents of the tub were for reversing the spell.

Eyvind was tempted to immerse the rock into it but couldn't take that chance. There was still time for him to find a solution.

He read the list of ingredients needed for the transformation—most made no sense at all and contained some items he had never heard of. He was frustrated with this turn of events and looked around. The metal tub again caught his eye. The temptation to set the rock into its mucky contents crossed his mind, and yet again, he resisted. He didn't know what exactly that brew was. It could be something that could damage Roni permanently.

Eyvind tried to convince himself that he could try to assemble the items needed for the spell and do it himself. The spell required that the concoction cook for several hours before it was ready for use. He wasn't sure he had the time. He was in a dilemma now.

Raidon broke Eyvind's concentration by bursting in to warn him.

"We better leave now, Eyvind. I can hear horses at a distance. They'll be here soon. Any luck?" he asked, looking around.

Eyvind sat unmoved on the chair, holding the Book of Spells in one hand and the rock in the other. He didn't answer. He heard Raidon's warning but faced a tough decision.

"Sire!" Raidon tried to get his attention.

Eyvind nodded at Raidon. "Give me a few minutes. Keep watch until then and let me know when they're close by."

He was still uncertain about what he was going to do. The temptation to immerse the rock in the tub became increasingly strong, but he continued to resist the urge. He didn't want anything bad to happen to Roni, now that he had her so close by.

He caressed the stone in his hand gently and thought about taking the book with him and cooking the spell later.

But will I find the list of strange items that this spell demands? Maybe the ogre has them in this house. But it will take me time to look for the ingredients in this strewn mess. And time is one thing I don't have now. Aurelius and his thugs are upon us.

These thoughts swirled in his mind on a loop.

"Sire! No more. They are right here. We'll get caught if we remain here any longer. Let's leave." Raidon came back in again to warn him about the approaching party.

Eyvind nodded and rose from the chair and stood next to the tub, not wanting to place the rock into it, but at the last minute, he took a chance and gently dropped it into the muck.

He closed his eyes in mounting tension. *Have I done the right thing? Please let the stone become Roni.*

He then opened his eyes, knowing it was too late now because the stone was already submerged in the slimy contents.

At first, nothing occurred, but within a few moments, the whole tub began to glow brightly.

Raidon again burst in with a warning, but words died on his lips when he saw the glowing tub.

Both men stared at the spectacle and became lost in it.

The glow increased further, brightening the room, until it reached about the height of a person. They both wondered if it had worked. The luminescence began to subside, and the shape of a person emerged.

Eyvind was excited, but at the same time was afraid in case it was someone else who never should have been freed.

Raidon ran back out to see how close Aurelius and his men were, leaving Eyvind in the study.

As the figure began to take shape, the glow almost vanished.

Raidon ran back in to urge Eyvind to leave immediately. "Eyvind, if we don't leave right now, we may have to fight it out—"

He stopped short as he stared at the image in front of him. It was someone dressed in strange warrior regalia complete with a helmet that concealed the face.

Eyvind was livid. He feared the worst, and there was nothing he could do now. He had released a monster.

They both searched the surroundings for anything they could use as a weapon to defend themselves against the warrior.

The warrior in turn looked at them in alarm, and before they got a chance to grab something off the floor, a voice yelled out, "Stop! It's me!"

They were taken aback.

The warrior removed the helmet and unveiled the face. It was indeed she. Roni.

"We need to leave now," urged Raidon. Before he exited the chamber, he stopped to look at Roni standing in the room. Puzzled and relieved, he departed the chamber to keep a lookout for Aurelius.

At first, Eyvind hesitated, but understanding the urgency to make haste, he grabbed her hand, yanked her out of the tub, and negotiated his way through the clutter.

They rushed through room after room until they reached the front door where they found Raidon pressed against the wall next to the door and joined him.

The galloping horses could be heard close by.

They looked around to figure out how they were going to make their escape.

Aurelius and his men had nearly reached the ogre's house.

Eyvind suddenly realized he had left the Book of Spells in the study.

He released his grip on Roni's hand and ran back into the depths of the lair to retrieve the book. But before he departed, he removed the vial from around his neck and gave it to Roni. He had almost forgotten about it.

She looked at it in complete surprise because, until that moment, she had not realized it was gone from around her neck.

"Sire! Where're you going?" asked Raidon in a panic.

"Don't worry. I forgot the Book of Spells. Just leave without me if you have to," he yelled back.

Raidon was distressed by Eyvind's instructions. He couldn't possibly leave him behind. However, the thunder of horses was even closer, and now they could be seen emerging from the woods.

ON THE OTHER SIDE of the forest, Aurelius and his men were preparing to accost the crazed woodcutter after hearing an enormous ruckus echoing through the woods.

Aarrggghhh....

They spread out and fanned the area until they saw a small cottage butted up against the hillock, and in the distance, they could hear loud grunts and ramblings.

They followed the groans until they saw an inhumanly large creature, tall and awkward, with a disproportionately large head and shining golden-yellow eyes lumbering through the trees. The soldiers came to a standstill and halted in their tracks. They didn't know said maladroit creature was actually just about to set out on his search for a Roni-sized pebble, the same Imen woman these men were in search of. Looking at the scene before them, they were left agape, as they had never imagined the woodcutter could be so menacing.

"I-I think that's the woodcutter, Sire," commented one of the soldiers, hesitantly.

Aurelius was filled with excitement but also felt a tinge of apprehension as he had not expected such a brutish creature. However, he signaled his men to rush ahead and catch the ogre off guard when the creature was making his way into the forest.

Bomo was indeed caught by surprise as he found himself detained by the soldiers, who circled him with their swords drawn.

Aurelius then questioned him exhaustively regarding the whereabouts of the potion he'd acquired from Laris.

"Where is the vial you pilfered off the Imperial Knight?"

"Who? Wot vial? I don't know such a Knight."

"Do you know what is the penalty for slaying a Knight? Be warned. I will gladly drive my sword into your chest if your answer displeases me."

Hearing the threat to his life, the awkward dimwit wasted little time in confessing everything about the vial and how it had shattered and splashed against the rock wall.

"Show me the cut rocks with gold specks in them. Take us to your gold pile."

Bomo hesitated. He didn't want to show these men his gold hoard. But as greedy as he was for the gold, he knew he would have to make the difficult choice to part with the gold-speckled rocks from the cave walls and give it to Aurelius in hopes of having his life spared.

Aurelius smirked when Bomo took his time to decide.

Little did Bomo know Aurelius' avarice for gold surpassed his own, and the royal minister was not going to let this opportunity go. He didn't need the ogre's permission to take the gold. He was going to help himself to whatever he wanted, regardless.

This became evident to Bomo immediately, seeing the man's lips twist in a sneer, and he knew he had to outdo himself in order to save his thick hide.

"I can do somethin' better, Sire. I am not just a woodcutter but also a sorcerer. Great sorcerer. You 'ave no idea what magic I can do. I can make people disappear. I 'ave turned an Imen into a rock. And I alone 'ave power to change her back whenever I want. Now I can ask her for anything I want."

Aurelius salivated at the thought of having captured a sorcerer who was surprisingly full of talent. He couldn't have wished for something better. He was in the advantage, having a sure thing in his possession. A sorcerer. And now the opportunity to capture an Imen. He knew he could easily discard the sorcerer after he learned everything he wanted from him. And he would keep the Imen forever. What a fortune it would be—imagining an Imen at his beck and call.

"Tell me everything. All secrets. Every single revelation, big or small."

Bomo kept shifting his weight from one foot to the other, reluctant to reveal it all but was forced to do so. The beast disclosed it all, except for his secret hoard of gold that lay hidden beneath the floor of his study.

Aurelius pondered the matter for just a couple of seconds and decided to come back to the cottage for the gold after the woodcutter retrieved the Imen Callioux. The Imen was decidedly more important. The greedy minister ordered the beast to take them to where he had transformed her to stone.

Bomo fearfully led them to the spot where he had cast the spell on Roni, and after a long, empty search, he picked up a couple of stones that he thought could be the "one."

Aurelius was frustrated with Bomo and unimpressed thus far. "How can you not be sure? You are supposed to be a great sorcerer. How can you not identify the right one?"

"Let me go back to me house, and I show how I transform stone I 'ave collected into Imen." He used all his sub-intelligence to fight to save his own hide and try to convince Aurelius, as he recognized Aurelius' lust for gold and sorcery and tried to use it to his advantage.

"Once you 'ave Imen in captivity, you can ask for as much gold as you can possibly want."

Intoxicated by visions of unlimited wealth and power, the minister granted the clod a chance to prove himself.

Bomo was quite proud of himself for having talked his way out, but deep inside, he feared the inability to deliver the promises.

As they rode back to his lair, he searched his pocket for the rocks he'd selected and held them in his hand one by one and hoped one of them was Roni.

He quietly called out to his mother in the afterlife and pleaded with her for help even though he knew it was futile. He had gotten himself into a precarious situation from which he could not extricate himself easily.

Bomo seriously lacked the wit and intelligence to craft a plan that could give him a way out. The ogre cursed himself and searched his tiny brain for a plan if one of the rocks failed to transform into Roni.

They rode through the forest at full gallop and approached Bomo's lair. Piles of wood remained scattered around, and nothing seemed amiss.

It wasn't until they approached the front door that Bomo's heart sank. The door had been forced open.

At first, Aurelius didn't take much notice of it since the whole place was chaotic. It wasn't until he saw the expression on Bomo's face that he asked, "What's the matter, woodcutter?"

Bomo was speechless. He was consumed with an ominous feeling he had been robbed of all his hard work.

Me gold. Me secret hoard. All gone. Now wot am I supposed to do?

All those years, he'd toiled hard, hauling load after load of wood to amass his gold stash, and now it was all gone in one fell swoop. The specimen could hardly move. He was seized with blind terror and a strange sort of panic, something he had never encountered before.

Aurelius became impatient with him and poked him with his horsewhip. "What happened? What's wrong?"

Bomo offered no answer. He cautiously pushed the door open and shuffled his way in.

"Woodcutter, you better not come up empty because I will string you up dry and hang you from the nearest tree and leave you to die. Do you understand? Don't try to play me for a fool. I need that Imen. And where's the gold you took from the cave?" Aurelius threatened menacingly.

Bomo quietly trudged his way through his home, encased in dread, as he entered room after room and finally, made his way to the study.

Aurelius looked around, taking in the broken furniture and the burlap sacks tacked to the windows, and seeing the space from the inside, he was amazed at how big the dwelling actually was. He had no idea that it extended into the hillock.

At last, they entered the study, and Bomo became anxious because he was certain, beyond a shadow of a doubt, that his secret stash had been looted.

In a corner of the study, the pile of golden rubble sat exactly where he had left it.

Aurelius promptly had his men haul it away and secure it. Bomo was never going to see a shard of it.

Aurelius then shoved the ogre down, making him fall to the ground close to the compartment that lay hidden under the floor.

Bomo couldn't believe it. Through the cracks in the wooden flooring, his secret stash seemed to be untouched, but he couldn't be sure. The furniture and piles of books remained in the same state of disarray above it.

However, the only way he could be certain was if he examined it for himself. And he could not do so unless all these men left him alone. He had to find a way to get out of Aurelius' grip and check his hoard. Bomo became restless, his anxiety rising.

Meanwhile, looking around the shambolic chamber, Aurelius saw the books that had been flung around as well as the cauldron lying on its side.

His eyes moved to the tub sitting on the floor with the mucky content. The ground had wet footprints leading away from the tub and exiting the chamber.

Aurelius was furious. He struck Bomo with his horsewhip repeatedly as the lout lay on the floor where he had fallen, yelling, "Get up, you fool! You have the wrong stones! Someone's already been here and transformed your Imen. Look!" He pointed to the footprints.

Bomo clumsily rose to his feet as fast as he could to see what Aurelius was ranting about. Indeed, there they were—footprints that clearly belonged to a woman approximately Roni's size. He looked around his chamber like a dumbfounded imbecile who couldn't believe what he was seeing.

"'Ow'd you know it's 'er?" he asked Aurelius.

"Who do you think they belong to? Your mother?" the man screamed out, pointing with his whip at the footprints, that were quickly drying.

Bomo was stunned. He reached into his pocket and produced the rocks he was carrying and looked at them in disappointment.

Aurelius grabbed them from his hand in a fit of rage and threw them into the tub. They landed with a loud clang into the mucky liquid.

Both Bomo and Aurelius stared at the tub, hoping for a miracle, but nothing occurred.

They remained in their frozen state until Aurelius barked out his order. "Soldiers, follow these footprints before they dry and disappear. I want this Imen captured alive. You understand? Alive. I want her now!"

The soldiers went to work, following the damp footprints out of the chamber and through the rooms, but they had dried and disappeared by the time they moved through the first two.

"They've disappeared, Sire," reported one of the soldiers.

Aurelius was ready to strike someone dead in fury. "Then comb the forest and look for them! They couldn't have gone too far," he shouted.

"They, Sire?" asked the soldier.

"Yes, they! It is obvious someone brought her here and released her from her state. Now, go and search for her and the rest of the culprits!" he screamed, unable to believe the kind of dimwits he had in his army.

Bomo was now worried for his own life. He could not predict Aurelius' next move. For all he knew, the minister was going to kill him there and then. Before he could formulate any plan in the lone cell of his tiny brain, Aurelius turned to him, drew his sword out, and pointed it at the clumsy bumpkin.

"Now, you're going to tell me who else was there and how many saw you cast your spell upon her."

Bomo became nervous and couldn't think of what to say or do. He began to mumble and stutter an incoherent garble.

"Speak now!" demanded Aurelius.

"I-I-I… I'm not sure," he replied anxiously.

"Then think hard, or I'll drive this blade through your thick head, and maybe that'll help you remember," he pressured him as he pushed the tip of the sword a little harder until a bead of blood oozed out.

Bomo didn't want to lose his life or his gold hoard. "I-I remember now. There was someone who distracted me when I was chasing the Imen and taking aim. But I don't know who. I was trying to turn her to stone, so I didn't see who diverted me mind."

Aurelius felt his fury blaze through his body. He held the sword firmly against Bomo's chest and became ready to drive it through him.

"Wait!" pleaded Bomo as he held his hands out in front. "Wait. I'm a sorcerer, and I know many spells and secrets that you'd want to know. I could 'elp you get another one easily," he bargained.

Unconvinced, Aurelius held his blade firmly pressed against Bomo's skin, but his lust for spells and magical things superseded everything else.

"I-I can do it. I promise. I-I can give you another Imen. I 'ave many spells," the ogre stuttered his plea to Aurelius, willing to promise him anything and everything if it saved his life.

Eventually, Aurelius succumbed to Bomo's requests.

"I want you to find and deliver an Imen to me immediately. I'm running out of patience, and if you fail me this time, I'll have your head on a stake," commanded Aurelius.

Bomo knew this was an unattainable request since he didn't know where to find an Imen, where they lived, or how to lure one.

"Well? What are you thinking about? You better deliver on your promises. Don't underestimate me or test my patience."

Bomo found himself in more trouble than he could have ever imagined. His eyes flitted around the room, hoping to find a solution to his problem. But nothing came to him. He was done for, as there was simply no way out of this situation. He looked around the study that lay in a complete state of disarray and was suddenly seized with anxiety when he searched for the Book of Spells.

Bomo rushed to his table and moved things around to look for it, and his actions immediately caught Aurelius' attention.

"What're you looking for now?" he asked.

Bomo gave no reply.

Aurelius became enraged. "Answer me! What're you looking for?" he repeated threateningly.

"Me book. It's gone," replied Bomo despondently.

"What book?" Aurelius barked out.

"She stole it! She took it!" he yelled out. Bomo's mind had gone wild. The thought of losing his precious Book of Spells was unendurable. It was all gone: the Book of Spells as well as Roni.

He was finished. He was sure he was as good as dead. The ogre quickly came back to reality when he felt something poke him at his side.

Aurelius had his blade out and was pushing it firmly against Bomo's flesh.

"Are you telling me it's all lost? What good are you to me now?" yelled Aurelius.

Bomo could not believe his luck. He had just pleaded for his life, and now he was back to square one. What was he going to tell him now in order to have his life spared?

"You're of no use to me!" Aurelius barked out in disgust as he prepared to drive the sword deep into his chest.

Bomo grabbed the blade with his thick hands and pleaded for his life one more time. He tried a last-ditch effort to bargain for his miserable existence. Besides, he needed to check for his gold, and he couldn't do it if he were dead. The thought of having worked so hard for his hoard of gold, only to have it slip away so suddenly filled him with panic.

Bomo felt wretched. He searched his cranium for a bargaining chip to buy his way out, but he was running out of time.

Aurelius tried to push hard on his sword to drive it into him, but Bomo held the blade with his hands and tried to shove it away.

His hands began to bleed as Aurelius twisted the blade. Bomo yelled out in a loud cry, "I know the spells by 'eart an' if you kill me, you'll never find out!"

Aurelius was not convinced because so far, the specimen had come up empty. However, his greed for power and gold drove him to let the pressure off and lower his weapon.

Bomo let go of the blade and looked at his bleeding hands. The calluses on his palms were so thick from wielding an axe for so many years that the blade had barely made superficial cuts across his skin.

His heart raced fast and continued to pound hard as he pondered the uncertainty of his life that now hung from a fragile thread.

The avarice for gold and riches plagued Aurelius, and the grip it had on him was overwhelming. Although his instincts gnawed at him and told him the ogre might just be a bumbling idiot, he went against his better judgment and believed him once again.

Aurelius returned the blade to its sheath and kicked Bomo in the abdomen. He expected him to go flying backward; however, the beast remained rigid like a pillar.

Bomo could have easily crushed Aurelius, but it was the rest of his party that kept him from doing so. The cheek of this man to have kicked Bomo.

Aurelius paced the ransacked chamber in deep frustration and warned Bomo one last time.

"You'd best know the spells and be able to find me an Imen, or there won't be a next time."

Bomo breathed a sigh of relief and realized his life was no longer going to be the same from this point forth.

Aurelius was now the keeper of his destiny.

The crazed minister exited the chamber in complete disgust, leaving Bomo alone inside. Each step Aurelius took was burdened with frustration and anger as he went out to see if the soldiers had any luck tracking the footprints.

As he came upon them, he could tell from the expressions on their faces they hadn't found anyone. No words could express the rage that flowed through Aurelius' veins. He had lost all his opportunities, and the only hope remaining lay with the imbecile yokel.

"Search the forest for her! Don't just stand there and expect me to do all the thinking!" he yelled out.

"But, Sire, I have three men combing the forest already, and I don't think it's safe to send out more," replied the leader timidly.

Aurelius stopped short of ordering the rest of them to join the search when he thought about his own safety if he were left alone with the ogre. He concealed his cowardice by replying, "Safety? He's just a woodcutter. Very well, let me know as soon as possible."

The soldier refrained from giving an answer, fearing the consequences. It was clear they feared for their own lives, especially since the ogre proclaimed himself to be a sorcerer.

The coward nervously looked back at Bomo's lair and became anxious about reentering it alone. He ordered one of his men to accompany him in case the brute thought about fleeing through a secret passageway.

The accompanying soldier knew better. They both disappeared into the lair, whilst the rest kept watch outside.

The soldiers grumbled amongst each other about Aurelius' cowardliness and their frustrations with him, and as they did so, they heard the gallop of horses taking off in a direction away from them. They ran around to see what was happening and noticed all their horses had fled into the forest.

They chased after them, but the beasts were in full gallop and soon vanished into the dense foliage. They looked at one another in complete disbelief and wondered how all of them could have managed to get loose. After all, they were tied securely.

They ran back to see if the culprits were still there, and upon reaching where the horses were tied, they were met by Aurelius, who had dashed outside to investigate the commotion.

"The horses, Sire. The horses got loose," confessed one of the soldiers breathlessly, knowing he was the one about to face the minister's ire.

Aurelius was perplexed at first, but he immediately turned his attention to the area where the horses had been tied. It was empty. The man was right. Not a single one remained.

"Who unhitched them? How'd they get away? Answer now or heads will roll" he lashed out in fury.

"It wasn't us, Sire. We just heard them take off into the woods," replied one timidly in a soft voice.

"They made off with the horses right before your eyes, and none of you saw a thing?" he barked out sarcastically.

"There were no riders, and we didn't see anyone around, Sire. It's just very strange," explained another.

"Sorcery!" exclaimed Aurelius. He ran back into the lair to demand an explanation from the woodcutter.

MEANWHILE, IN THE PALACE, soon after Aurelius had departed with Eyvind and Raidon to search for the ogre and the Imen, King Audun gathered his closest confidants to summon the main dignitaries and prefects representing all regions of Carron for an emergency council meeting.

Worry besieged him as he stood facing the daunting task of selling them a tale that could pose to be challenging amongst a crowd of shrewd men. Had it been anyone other than Eyvind, it wouldn't have presented half the challenge.

Eyvind was loved and cherished by most and had virtually no enemies. However, this was a dark age—a time when good virtues were considered archaic, and moralities were just romantic notions that represented a distant past. Eyvind was a living reminder of that past.

In this day and age, greed and corruption drove the cogs of this nation and produced immense momentum toward success. There was an insatiable avarice for the acquisition of wealth and power at any cost. It was hard to believe any nation was able to maintain its secrecy, given the level of greed that pervaded the lands.

Almost anyone could be bought for the right price. Ordinary people were promised wealth and benefits by the authorities in return for their loyalties and support. Bribes and corruption were the backbone upon which everything was built and operated.

Yet, these were the very things Eyvind deplored and refused to be a part of. He had a unique and special way of winning the trust and agreement of others.

His father, however, knew no other method than bribery in order to get his way. If that failed, there were other more nefarious means of achieving his goals and getting the cooperation of his people.

It didn't take long to assemble the requested parties as they made their way to the King's private chamber in the High Keep. It was a large circular room with windows all around, giving an impressive three-hundred-and-sixty-degree view of Carron.

The entrance to it was through the floor from the room below. The chamber itself had sparse furnishings. A large round table sat at the center upon which lay a few stacks of old volumes and rolled-up atlases.

A large map lay spread on the table, depicting the circular landmass of Atlantis cut into four quadrants by large rivers flowing in the four cardinal points. Their land lay on the northeast quadrant. Atlantis was in the center of the earth.

Various writing implements, charts, looking glasses of different sizes, and mapping instruments were scattered about the table. The only other piece of furniture in this place was a massive regal-looking, straight-backed chair. With no fireplace, and windows all around, the room was bitterly cold all the time. A heavy bearskin rug covered the icy stone floor beneath the table, buffering them from the effects of the frigid chamber.

It was obvious this was not a place for creature comforts. This space served a crucial purpose, allowing the King and his men to confer privately in matters of the land.

The coterie of prefects and other dignitaries ascended the cold steps into the chamber in single file. The space was soon filled with the occupants—most of whom had never been invited to this private sanctum. The men were puzzled by the request. No one knew why King Audun had summoned them.

Moments later, the King arrived and cast his cold eyes upon the attendees, taking in the expressions on their faces. Without saying a word, he sat down ramrod straight upon the regal chair. Even while being seated, Audun still seemed to tower over his men by the sheer strength of his persona. Not a single thought spread across his features, giving him time to compose the narrative that was going to be delivered in this room.

A shiver of apprehension rolled across the chamber when the dignitaries couldn't seem to get a read on their King.

At long last, the suspense ended when Audun proceeded to spin his web of lies, in a matter-of-fact tone.

"Prefects, there's a reason for your audience in this High Keep. It's the only place where secret matters can be discussed in confidence."

"Secret matters?" The men whispered the word while looking at one another and then at their King. They were all ears now, not missing a single mysterious note in Audun's voice. The tension in the room could be cut with a knife, and suspense built up, taut like a drum. Silence pervaded the room, making some of the men hold their breath, fearing they might miss something important.

The men crept closer and huddled around the table, closing the gaps as tightly as they could with those at the back pressed up against the ones in the front. With mounting tension in the room, no one dared to utter a word or interrupt, even though they had the sudden uncontrollable urge to shout out their questions all at once.

Audun was cunning enough to let the suspense build a little longer before he continued. He needed his men's acceptance of the nefarious task which he had already begun.

"Yes. Secret matters. Do I need to warn you that anything discussed in this chamber holds the penalty of death if a word of it is uttered outside these walls to anyone who's not privy?" he began.

They stared at him blankly and agreed to keep their lips sealed with a nod of their heads. He rose from his chair and paced back and forth as he tried to formulate his dialogue.

"What sort of secret matters are we talking about?" asked one of the prefects who couldn't stand the suspense any longer.

Audun raised his hand in the air to gesture for silence.

"Eyvind renounced his right to the throne," he began in a regretful tone.

With that one line, the restless chatter and uproar among the assembled men prevented him from speaking further

"Silence!" cried out one of Audun's closest advisors.

The room once again fell silent. The men were puzzled by Eyvind's action.

He is the heir. Why would he do such a thing? The hopes of the people of Carron rested with him and his marriage to Adina.

"Eyvind chose to make that decision after a plot to sabotage this union was uncovered by Laris, who now lies dead in the house of worship!" Audun exclaimed as he pounded his fist on the heavy table.

Not a single soul stirred. They were riveted by the news.

A dead Knight? This was worse than the things they had imagined. *What was next?*

The dignitaries were waiting for the second sword to fall upon their necks, and at the same time, like starving fish in a tiny pond waiting for the first crumb of food, they were hungrily anticipating the next bit of news that would reach their ears.

"Laris? Laris is dead?" they asked in disbelief.

"Why would he do such a thing at a time like this?" asked several others.

"Doesn't make sense."

"Eyvind is in Aurelius' custody, who, as a matter of fact, has gone to root out the rest of Eyvind's cohorts and prevent them from carrying out this coup d'etat. We can never be complacent about anything!"

The prefects were in shock. Eyvind and treason? They couldn't equate the two in their minds. This was more than they had expected.

All of them were left speechless, with their brains having lost the ability to string two sentences together.

"My own son was seeking to sabotage this pact right under my nose! Had we not uncovered his wretched plan, we would be facing a civil war now. As it is, we have breached our security…to some degree…by inviting the Carthinians into Jasper, but there was no other way around that," he explained.

His audience was riveted by his dialogue.

"How long have we strived for this pact? Five years! Five years, Prefects! And it wasn't until we compromised ourselves by allowing them into Jasper that they agreed to go through with it. Don't think for a moment I don't fret about having the enemy crawling around my citadel and probing for vulnerabilities.

"All this hard work while my son...my flesh and blood…was plotting to overthrow me and take the throne by force so he could carry out his agenda. My very own flesh and blood!" he shouted in angered passion, shaking his head. Though lies, the words still rang true across the room in the way the King delivered them. Betrayal and anger were apparent on his face, while his tone held the right amount of impassioned fervor.

The men were stunned by the news.

Silence filled the room, which was eventually broken by Prefect Rhine when he asked, "What is to become of this pact now?"

Prefect Rhine was an elderly man, who was in charge of a modest region of Carron. Those whom he represented held him responsible for every decision he made. Although he too was motivated by the lure of gold and riches, he tamed his aggressive drive, unlike the rest, and worked for his people.

He was much older than the rest, prudent and wiser too. Rhine used rationale to carefully weigh out the pitfalls against the benefits before making his decisions. Occasionally, the others abandoned his decisions and followed the lure of riches instead.

But it wasn't long before they discovered the snags that eventually cost them dearly in the long run. However, they never learned from their mistakes and continued to be seduced by greed, time and time again. It was as though the ramifications of their decisions failed to leave a single impression upon them.

But Rhine was not like them. To say the least, he was sagacious, and nothing could escape his eyes. The King had to be careful now while delivering the next piece of news.

"The pact? The pact remains unchanged. We proceed as planned," declared Audun.

"Begging your pardon, Your Highness… What about the marriage between Eyvind and Adina?" asked Rhine.

"Yes, yes. That's right. What about the marriage?" the others chimed in.

"Order, order!" shouted one of the advisors.

"The marriage will take place as planned, but it will be to Korin instead," Audun declared.

"I don't mean to sound naïve, but would Korin wed her without protest? You don't anticipate any objections from the Carthinians or Korin on this matter? It's quite a contrastive change and a sudden one at that," Rhine carefully pointed out the flaw in the plan.

The rest chimed in their concerns in a roar of questions following Rhine's comment. The senior advisor once again called for order until the chaotic dissonance subsided.

"You're right, Rhine. We are anticipating some discord over this from the Carthinians, but I'm convinced we can manage to sway them into doing the right thing. As for Korin, he'll have no objection to marrying Adina. Trust me," he replied. He paused and allowed his men to take in this news. He had to carefully step into the minefield that Eyvind's actions had left behind.

The prefects chatted and conferred in hushed tones about this new development and seemed deeply concerned. They lacked Audun's confidence in the new turn of events.

Audun sensed their concern and brought them to attention so he could quickly proceed without further uproar.

Before Audun spoke, he was interrupted by Prefect Banyon from the North-East province. This was one of the wealthiest provinces and a home, or a second home, to most of the noble and elite families of Carron.

Prefect Banyon was the son of a stablehand who rose from poverty to riches by joining the King's Cavalry. He quickly ascended the ranks to be knighted and put in charge of the entire cavalry of the North-East province.

He was charismatic and born with a silver tongue. He could sell anything to anyone without their blinking an eye. He secretly coveted a life of riches and desired to be one of the elites. And it wasn't long before the wealthy noticed his penchant for finer things and began courting him for their greedy objectives. The man had the magnetism to convince people across the province to believe he was one of them.

To the common folk, he was a hero, whose achievements they were proud of, and in their eyes, he could do no wrong. To the elite, he was one among them, their comrade. Banyon was thus perfect in carrying out their dirty deeds of extracting more taxation from their subjects without an outcry or a threat of an upheaval.

The wealthy didn't waste time encouraging him to become prefect of their region and leave the cavalry. This presented itself as the opportunity of a lifetime, and Banyon seized it. He was immediately made the prefect.

He made lofty promises to the subjects and deceived them into working harder and surrendering more of their earnings, crops, goods, etc. for the "good of their nation."

He used the ploy of "bad-mouthing" the noble and the elite at every opportunity in order to diffuse any suspicions upon himself.

Covertly, he amassed his own fortune that was negotiated for him by those whom he served. Banyon was a puppet who carried out the wishes and whims of the elite, but the threat of exposure of his true intentions and actions was ever-present in daily reminders sent to him by his masters. He was a low and despicable individual who snugly fit into his deplorable niche, someone whom they could squash like a bug.

Banyon went on to ask, "Your Highness? What would prompt Eyvind to plan an overthrow when he was already the heir?"

This was a plausible question that set the tiny gears in everyone's heads in motion as they too wondered the same thing. Suddenly the idea of wanting to overthrow the King seemed a little absurd, especially given the timing.

Audun's advisors leaned toward him and whispered into his ear.

Meanwhile, Banyon continued, "It just seems odd to want to carry out such a plot at a time like this. Surely you don't plan such a siege when the enemy is in your house."

Audun was annoyed at being pushed into a corner to defend his lies with more lies.

"On the contrary, Prefect Banyon. The timing is excellent if you plan on killing two birds with one stone," he answered in annoyance.

"Whatever do you mean?" asked another prefect in alarm.

"If the heads of two powerful nations were simultaneously removed, then the chance of war is reduced to a minimum. It's quite brilliant if you ask me. It's easy to quash any resistance that may stand in the way. Wouldn't you think?" Audun disclosed.

"That is brilliant!" exclaimed some, nodding their heads.

"Very brazen of Eyvind. Didn't know he had it in him," said others, shock evident upon their faces.

"The Carthinians haven't become suspicious of this plot, have they?" asked another.

"We've taken every precaution to keep this from getting out. You're the first to hear about it, and I expect you to remain tight-lipped about it. I need not remind any one of you of the consequences," answered Audun sternly.

"What excuse was given to the Carthinians for Eyvind's bowing out?" asked another.

"None yet," replied Audun.

"None? Then how can we be sure they would stomach this information without suspicion?" asked another.

"Trust me, they will stomach it far better than you have," answered Audun.

"I don't understand," returned the same prefect.

Audun did not want to disclose everything, but he found himself compelled to divulge more than he had intended.

"Korin and Adina are already acquainted with one another if you must know," he stated abruptly.

A roar filled the room as the news took everyone by surprise. Questions poured forth.

"How can that be?" they asked. They were deeply puzzled.

"Are Camden and Tara aware of this?" asked others.

"I'm not certain," replied the King.

"That's unnerving," stated another.

"If there's one thing I can assure you, Korin is not one to reveal his identity to anyone indiscriminately," he barked back.

"But, Your Highness, Korin obviously knows who she is, right?" asked another eager prefect.

Audun did not want to assume anything, especially having not spoken to Korin directly. He had to be careful of his comments and project confidence. He came to his son's defense with his words. "Of course, Korin knew she was part of the royal court. He has been using her to spy on the Carthinians."

The prefects were amazed at Korin's shrewdness and somewhat awed.

"Impressive!" many shouted.

"For the sake of caution, what if the Carthinians do sense something amiss? After all, this is profound news and not something that one can ignore under the pretense of minor glitches," replied Prefect Rhine.

"Like I said, we're prepared to deal with the Carthinians and have anticipated their posturing. This pact will go forth, and everything will go on as planned," Audun replied, raising his voice.

"But how can we be so certain? Frankly, I would have extreme mistrust of the whole matter if I were in their stead," argued Rhine.

"Well, you're not in their stead, and I'm telling you they'll agree to our terms. We need this to happen, as there won't be another chance," he growled out again.

"But why are we so anxious about signing a peace pact with them? Aside from access to the sea, Carthinia is a wasteland. We've lived happily without needing them, so why this sudden urgency for a pact? Maybe someone else has a better insight and may want to take the liberty to tell me because it has never made sense to me whatsoever," stated Prefect Rhine in complete frankness.

"Is this really about peace? I know it has a nice ring to it—peace with our neighbors. But we have never adhered to it, just managed a semblance of it. So, he's right, Sire. Why the urgency?" asked another prefect.

Just then, several others joined in with their concerns regarding the true nature of this peace pact, and it wasn't long before most of them started questioning the true motive.

Audun now faced a crowd who was sinking into doubt and suspicion, even against him. He had to act quickly if he wanted to save his plan and culminate the meeting before it moved into a different direction.

He thought fast as he used his command over the words and pummeled them where it affected the most. "Let me ask you if anyone here knows the true meaning of peace?" he began in a calm but defensive tone. "Can anyone tell me what that means? Or even what it means to live in peace?"

They all stared at him blankly. No one was sure where this conversation was going.

"You have families, neighbors, and acquaintances. How well do you get along with any of them? Well?" he asked, glaring at them.

No one answered. They looked puzzled.

"We've seen it all: bitter feuds with families, friends, and one another. If you cannot live in peace with those close to you and who are alike—those with whom you share your real world every day—then how can you possibly live in peace with those who are complete strangers, enemies, and different from us?" he preached ardently, driving his point into everyone's minds.

The prefects tacitly agreed with his statement.

"As long as suspicion, mistrust, jealousy, differences, dislikes, hatred, and a desire to covet things exist, there can never be peace. EVER! It's a novel and romantic idea for fools. So, allow me to tell you what peace is..."

The prefects were riveted to every word that poured out from Audun's mouth.

"Peace is a pawn in the game of WAR!" the King stated, pounding his fist on the heavy table, his voice laced with conviction. "It's nothing more and nothing less. It is a game piece used for strategy, and that strategy is to win. It's just that—a meaningless word that serves only the strong and plays on the emotions of the weak and fickle."

By this time, the men were mesmerized by his speech and wanted to know more.

Where is their King going with this? They wondered while nodding their heads.

"We'll conquer and decimate those who stand in our way. That's how we'll achieve 'true peace.' We're on a path to make our nation the strongest and the most powerful one in the entire quadrant," he stated with exuberance, smashing his hand down on the heavy desk.

The prefects nodded in agreement and waited for more with bated breath. They were now perfectly aligned with his way of thinking, even those who would have opposed it on a normal day.

"We'll paralyze those who pose a threat or stand in our way. With this pact, I plan on taking over Bodon using Carthinia to bear the casualties. And after that's accomplished, we'll take over Carthinia and quash them once and for all. Only then will we have peace. Capitulation to our superiority will render true peace!" he exclaimed after delivering his stemwinder speech.

The silence was deafening. Everyone was stunned by his comments. *How true!* They nodded in agreement, immediately understanding Audun's actions. Now it all made sense.

"To peace!" they chanted in unison.

They were astounded by his brilliant plan, although they were not yet privy to the details. Carron's superiority gleamed through. They were in awe. They bowed simultaneously, communicating their commitment to his plans and their loyalties to him.

Audun was pleased. By now, everyone had completely forgotten about Eyvind and the coup. They were intoxicated with the mirage of riches that danced before their eyes.

Prefect Millor was the most ruthless of all when it came to amassing wealth, and naturally, he was the first to speak up.

"Sire, how much wealth do we hope to plunder? And how will it be carved out?" His greed for gold was well known.

Audun had anticipated his question but cringed at the thought of being put on the spot yet again. Millor was not exactly his favorite prefect.

"It's premature to discuss plunder at this time, Prefect Millor. I'm sure we'll have plenty of time to go over the details as the plan proceeds. One thing I can assure each one of you is that you'll be richly rewarded for your efforts. This plan was not brewed overnight. It took five years to reach this point, and the plunder will not be disappointing," he replied while restraining his annoyance.

They were like a pack of hungry wolves salivating at the thought of the prey dangling before their mouths. Leave alone the actual work that needed to be done to catch the prey. They could smell and taste the wealth this endeavor would yield. The intensity with which they reached for something they knew little about or the risks involved was astounding.

Intoxicated by the possibility of making incredible fortunes, the leeches were restless about their share of the plunder. One question rose foremost in their minds.

Will I get an equal slice as my neighbor? Will the King favor some over the others?

But these thoughts were soon smothered under their greed. Their fervor and excitement continued to fuel their avarice and keep them going for a while until Audun swore each of them to an oath of secrecy.

"I forbid you to ever talk about this conversation with anyone. In case you do, you will be charged with treason and will have to face the same fate as Eyvind and his supporters. Think about the wealth you will be amassing once the plan is executed." These words were enough to seal their lips forever.

"Prefects, I expect your explicit and implicit support in this endeavor," he insisted.

"Hail Audun!" they shouted in unison, with their right hands pressed firmly against their hearts in loyalty to him.

The assembly adjourned, and everyone departed, silent and lost in their thoughts, initially. As they descended the stairs to reach the floor below, their questions and doubts arose, as heard in their mumbling to one another about the details. They clawed for news, wanting to find out as much information as possible. But no one knew any more than the other.

AND THUS, THE *RUTHLESS* intensified their *Pursuit* for the Imen, and rushed forward with their plans of conquest in usurping another nation, as well as plundering all the gold of Bodon.

To be continued…

Volume Three, Imen of Atlantis: Pursuit

ATLANTIS, DEFINING THE TERRITORY

ONCE UPON A TIME, at the center of the world, then known as Earthia, lay the mystical lands of Atlantis. The pulse of Earthia originates here—the kernel of all life origin.

Arranged in a circular fashion, as if pre-decreed, it is not one single landmass as would be assumed, but four large land masses separated by four rivers flowing in the four cardinal directions enveloping a separate central island. It was as if these land masses were the guardians of the secret hidden at the core.

To add to its protection, the central island is surrounded by a whirlpool fed by the currents of the four large rivers. The rules of nature don't seem to apply here. The waters of each river flow in both directions, inward and outward. This dangerous whirlpool possesses the power to suck in and drown any enemies who may think to plunder its secrets. These waters cannot be navigated by the sturdiest of ships or the most experienced of captains.

With so many guardians around this central island, you would think it has enfolded within itself many untold riches, but that is not so. This island is unique—uninhabited, with nothing growing upon it. Only a lone feature stands strong and tall, as if touching the skies and asking for its favor. A gigantic, towering black rock with a strong magnetic property, influenced only by the sun and moon.

A natural flow of power coexists in this dimension between the tides created worldwide in the water bodies and the celestial masses that interact with them. There is a constant tug-of-war of power within them.

The magnetic power of this rock draws in the waters of all Earthia toward the central whirlpool based on the position of the sun. As the sun encircles Earthia, the tides also move in the same direction, creating the ebbs and flows. The sun energizes the tower on whatever side is bathed with its energy, thereby causing the river closest to the sun-bathed side to draw the waters inwards toward the whirlpool.

The moon works against all this and conversely weakens the magnetic pull on the moon-bathed side, making the water flow outward, back into Earthia. These four water bodies thusly work hard, moving volumes of water in or out throughout the day, depending on the time and the position of the celestial bodies.

Each quadrant of Atlantis is walled by tall, unbroken mountain ranges along their outermost edges with the exception of the northeast quadrant.

Therein lies the difference. The Irrian Mountains that form the outer edge, cut diagonally through this quadrant leaving a generous swath of land sweeping freely against the outer sea. The outer sea encircling Atlantis is called the Velvet Sea and the four cardinal rivers cut through it flowing out into Earthia.

Upon this northeast quadrant, there are several nations. The nation of Carthinia is located on the entire swath of land that sweeps towards the Velvet Sea. The narrowest tip of this triangular swath terminates in the northeast where the Irrian Mountain range begins its coastal border for the rest of the quadrant. Due to its coastal access, Carthinia has tactical advantages over its rival nation of Carron.

The Velvet Sea surrounding all four landmasses of Atlantis is mostly calm with near-still waters, hardly any wind, and very rarely stormy, making it difficult for ships to sail across it to reach Atlantis. Also, the deep channels of the four water bodies around the quadrants have rapid currents flowing inward and outward throughout the day, so anyone caught in these currents is doomed. Death meets them faster than they can turn back. This keeps out most outsiders.

In the north east direction off the coast of Carthinia lies a smaller island with magnetic properties called Marteen. Seldom does anyone venture to it, especially those who are evil. The energy from this island is so strong that it affects the wicked adversely, making it difficult for them to halt on its shores for even a few minutes. The good ones seem to bear the energy for longer periods of time.

The land of Carthinia has flowing landscapes, even the flora and fauna differ from the rest of the nations. The climate here is mild in winter and warm for the rest of the year. Quite different from the rest of the nations where they have different seasons.

Rolling hills of gold dotted with oak-like trees of ironwood extend from one end to the other. Lakes and streams are abundant as waters from the mountains flow down in serpentine rivulets, sweeping across the landscape, pooling in some areas to create lakes, and eventually, making their way into the Velvet Sea.

Carron is located within the enclosure of the Irrian Mountains which surrounds the rest of the landmass. It is lush with vegetation, forests, lakes, and streams that empty into the river Loki, the only river that flows on the southwest border of this land, along the inner edge of the Talbot Mountains. This range sweeps east and merges with the outer Irrian mountains on the easternmost side. The river Loki is fed by small streams and rivulets, increasing in size, as it moves toward its delta, cutting through the cracks in the Irrian Mountains.

The delta formed by the river Loki separates Carron from the mysterious nation of Bodon which dwells deep in the belly of the Irrian Mountains on its eastern side. The Bodonians are an elusive but fierce people, secluded from the rest. No one has ever penetrated this nation, as a labyrinth of tunnels leads anyone who attempts such a thing to their utter destruction. The layout of Bodon or any path in and out lies unknown. But it is rumored this nation is full of gold hidden deep within the rocks of its mountain range.

The small nation of Nia lies to the south of Carron, separated by the river Loki and is surrounded by mountains on nearly all sides. Both Carron and Nia have warm summers and cold winters with snow and extreme weather conditions at times. Other minor kingdoms too exist in this quadrant, but most people are unaware of them.

Distant lore of the Carronites bespoke of magical beings who once lived in their forests, right in the middle of their nation. No one has seen these beings for many generations, and the folktale mostly has died down regarding them. The mystical Imen.